Hans Brinker

or The Silver Skates

By MARY MAPES DODGE

Abridged by NORA KRAMER

Illustrated by DON ALBRIGHT

D1542300

SCHOLASTIC BOOK SERVICES

New York Toronto London Auckland Sydney

Special contents copyright © 1967 by Scholastic Magazines, Inc. This edition is published by Scholastic Book Services, a division of Scholastic Magazines, Inc. All rights reserved.

5th printing.............................November 1971

Printed in the U.S.A.

To My Father

JAMES J. MAPES

THIS BOOK

IS DEDICATED IN GRATITUDE

AND LOVE

Contents

1. Hans and Gretel

ON A BRIGHT DECEMBER MORNING long ago, two thinly clad children were kneeling upon the bank of a frozen canal in Holland.

The sun had not yet appeared, but the gray sky near the horizon shone crimson with the coming day. Most of the good Hollanders were still enjoying their placid morning naps.

Now and then some peasant woman, posing a well-filled basket on her head, came skimming over the glassy surface of the canal; or a husky boy, skating to his day's work in the town, cast a good-natured grimace toward the shivering pair as he flew along.

Meanwhile, with many a vigorous puff and pull, the brother and sister seemed to be fastening something on their feet — not skates, certainly, but clumsy pieces of wood narrowed and smoothed at their lower edge, and pierced with holes, through which were threaded strings of rawhide.

These queer-looking affairs had been made by the boy Hans. His mother was a poor peasant woman, too poor to buy skates. But rough as these were, they had given the children many a happy hour upon the ice. Now, with cold red fingers, our young Hollanders tugged at the strings.

In a moment the boy arose, and with a careless "Come on, Gretel," glided easily across the canal.

"Ah, Hans," called his sister plaintively, "this foot is not well yet. The strings hurt me on last market day, and now I cannot bear them tied in the same place."

"Tie them higher up then," answered Hans, as without looking at her he performed a wonderful cat's-cradle step on the ice.

"How can I? The string is too short."

Giving vent to a good-natured Dutch whistle, he steered toward her.

"You are foolish to wear such shoes, Gretel, when you have a stout leather pair. Your wooden shoes would be better than these."

"Why, Hans! Do you forget? The father threw my beautiful new shoes in the fire. I can skate with these, but not with my wooden ones. Be careful —"

Hans had taken a string from his pocket. He knelt beside her and proceeded to fasten her skate with all the force of his strong young arm.

"Oh! Oh!" she cried, in real pain.

"I'll fix it — never fear," he said, with sudden tenderness, "but quickly now; Mother will need us soon."

He took off his cap, removed the tattered lining, and adjusted it in a smooth pad over the top of Gretel's worn-out shoe. "Now!" he cried triumphantly, at the same time arranging the strings. "Can you bear some pulling?"

Gretel drew up her lips as if to say, "Hurt away." In another moment they were laughing together, as hand in hand they flew along the canal.

Presently, *squeak! squeak!* sounded beneath Hans's feet. Next his strokes grew shorter, ending with a jerk, and finally he lay sprawled on the ice.

"Ha! ha!" laughed Gretel, "that was a fine tumble!" But even as she laughed, she came, with a graceful sweep, close to her prostrate brother.

"Are you hurt, Hans? Oh, you are laughing! Catch me now" — and she darted away, shivering no longer, but with cheeks all aglow and eyes sparkling with fun.

Hans sprang to his feet and started in brisk pursuit. But before Gretel had traveled very far, her skates too began to squeak and she turned suddenly and skated into her pursuer's arms.

"Ha, ha! I've caught you!" cried Hans.

"Ha, ha! I caught *you*." she retorted, struggling to free herself.

Just then a clear, quick voice was heard calling "Hans! Gretel!"

"It's Mother," said Hans, looking solemn in an instant.

By this time the canal was gilded with sunlight,

and skaters were gradually increasing in numbers. It
was hard to obey, but Gretel and Hans quickly pulled
off their skates, leaving half the knots still tied.

Hans, with his great square shoulders and bushy
yellow hair, towered high above his blue-eyed little
sister as they trudged homeward. He was fifteen years
old; Gretel was nearly twelve. She was lithe and
quick, and her eyes had a dancing light in them.

As soon as the children turned from the canal, they
could see their parents' cottage. Their mother, in
jacket and petticoat and close-fitting cap, stood in the
crooked frame of the doorway.

If the cottage had been a mile away, it would still
have seemed near. In that flat country every object
stands out plainly in the distance. Indeed, were it not
for the dykes and the high banks of the canals, one
could stand almost anywhere in middle Holland without seeing a mound or a ridge between the eye and
the "jumping-off place."

Let me show you some of the curious things that
Hans and Gretel saw every day:

In Holland, or The Netherlands, as it is called today,
a large portion of the country is lower than the level
of the sea. Great dykes or banks have been erected to
keep the ocean where it belongs. Sometimes the dykes
give way, or spring a leak, with the most disastrous
results. They are high and wide, and the tops of some
of them are covered with buildings and trees. They

even have public roads on them, from which one may look down upon wayside cottages. Often the keels of floating ships are higher than the cottages, for many of the canals are higher than the land.

Ditches, canals, ponds, rivers, and lakes are everywhere to be seen. People are born, live, and die, and even have gardens, on the canalboats. The farmhouses, with roofs like great slouched hats pulled over their eyes, stand on wooden legs with a tucked-up sort of air, as if to say, "We intend to keep dry if we can." Even the horses wear a wide stool on each hoof to lift them out of the mire. It is a glorious country in summer for barefooted girls and boys — for wading, miniature ship sailing, rowing, fishing, and swimming!

Instead of green country lanes, green canals stretch from field to barn and from barn to garden. The farms, or polders, are merely great lakes pumped dry.

Great flapping windmills all over the land make it look as if flocks of huge sea birds were just settling upon it. There are hundreds of large windmills in Holland. They do many kinds of work, but their principal use is for pumping water from the lowlands into the canals.

The windmills are so constructed that they present their fans, or wings, to the wind in precisely the right direction to work. The miller may take a nap and feel quite sure that his mill will study the wind, and make the most of it, until he wakens. Every sail will spread itself to catch the faintest current of air. But in a heavy wind, they will shrink and hardly move.

In the spring there is always great danger of flooding. Then the rivers are choked with blocks of ice; they overflow before they can discharge their rapidly rising waters into the ocean. And with the sea chafing and pressing against the dykes, it is no wonder that Holland is often in a state of alarm. Engineers and workmen are stationed all along in threatened places, and a close watch is kept up night and day. When a general signal of danger is given, the inhabitants all rush to the rescue. Huge straw mats are pressed against the embankments, and fortified with clay and heavy stone. Once these are firmly in place, the ocean dashes against them in vain.

Raff Brinker, the father of Gretel and Hans, had for years been employed upon the dykes. One night in the midst of a terrible storm, in darkness and sleet, when the men were laboring at a weak spot near the Veermyk sluice, Raff fell from the scaffolding. He was taken home insensible, and from that hour he never worked again. Though he lived on, mind and memory were gone.

Gretel could not remember him otherwise than as a strange, silent man, whose eyes followed her vacantly whichever way she turned. But Hans had recollections of a hearty, cheerful-voiced father who was never tired of bearing him upon his shoulder, and whose careless song still seemed echoing near when Hans lay awake at night and listened.

2. The Silver Skates

DAME BRINKER earned a scanty support for her family by raising vegetables, spinning, and knitting. Once she had worked on board the barges plying up and down the canal, and had occasionally been harnessed with other women to the towing rope of a water dray, plying between Broek and Amsterdam. But when Hans had grown big and strong, he had insisted upon doing all such drudgery in her place. Besides, her husband had become so very helpless of late that he required her constant care. Although with less intelligence than a child, Raff was still strong of arm and very hearty, and Dame Brinker had sometimes great trouble in controlling him.

"Ah, children, he was so good and steady," she would say, "and as wise as a lawyer. Even the burgemeester would stop to ask him a question, and now alack! he doesn't know his wife and little ones. You remember the father, Hans, when he was himself — a great brave man — don't you?"

"Yes indeed, Mother, he knew everything and could do anything under the sun — and how he would sing! Why, you used to laugh and say it was enough to set the windmills dancing."

"So I did. Bless me, how the boy remembers! Gretel, child, take that knitting needle from your father, quick; he'll get it in his eyes maybe. And put the shoe on him. His poor feet are like ice half the time, but I can't keep 'em covered. All I can do —" and then Dame Brinker, sighing, would sit down and fill the low cottage with the whir of her spinning wheel.

Nearly all the outdoor work as well as the household chores were done by Hans and Gretel. At certain seasons of the year the children went out day after day to gather peat, which they stowed away in square, bricklike pieces, for fuel. At other times, when homework permitted, Hans rode the towing-horses on the canals, earning a few stivers a day; and Gretel tended geese for the neighboring farmers.

Hans was clever at carving in wood, and both he and Gretel were good gardeners. Gretel could sing, and sew, and run on great, high, homemade stilts better than any girl for miles around. She could learn a ballad in five minutes and find, in its season, any weed or flower you could name. But she dreaded books, and often the very sight of the figuring board in the old schoolhouse would set her eyes swimming, Hans, on the contrary, was slow and steady. The harder the task, whether in study or daily labor, the better he liked it. Boys who sneered at him out of school, on account of his patched clothes and scant leather breeches, were forced to yield him the post of honor in nearly every class.

It was only in winter months that Gretel and Hans could be spared to attend school; and for the past month they had been kept at home because their mother needed their services. Raff Brinker required constant attention now, and there was black bread to be made, the house to be kept clean, and stockings and other things to be knitted and sold at the market.

While they were busily assisting their mother on this cold December morning, a merry troop of girls and boys came skimming down the canal. There were fine skaters among them, and as the brightly clothed medley flitted by, it looked from a distance as though the ice had suddenly thawed and some gay tulip bed were floating along on the current.

There was the rich burgomaster's daughter, Hilda van Gleck, with her costly furs and loose-fitting green velvet sack; and, nearby, a pretty peasant girl, Annie Bouman, jauntily attired in a coarse scarlet jacket and a blue skirt just short enough to show her gray homespun hose. Then there was the proud Rychie Korbes, whose father, Mynheer van Korbes, was one of the leading men of Amsterdam; and, flocking closely around her, Carl Schummel, Peter and Ludwig van Holp, Jacob Poot, and a very small boy rejoicing in the tremendous name of Voostenwalbert Schimmelpenninck. There were nearly twenty other boys and girls in the party, and all seemed full of excitement and frolic.

Up and down the canal, within the space of a half mile they skated, exerting their racing powers to the utmost. Often the swiftest among them was seen to dodge from under the very nose of some pompous lawgiver or doctor, who with folded arms was skating leisurely toward the town.

Not only pleasure seekers and stately men of note were upon the canal. There were workpeople, with weary eyes, hastening to their shops and factories; market women with loads upon their heads; peddlers bending with their packs; bargemen with shaggy hair and wind-bleared faces, jostling roughly on their way; kind-eyed clergymen speeding perhaps to the bedsides of the dying; and, after a while, groups of children, with satchels slung over their shoulders, whizzing past toward the distant school. One and all wore skates excepting, indeed, a muffled-up farmer whose queer cart bumped along on the margin of the canal.

Before long the merry boys and girls were almost lost in the confusion of bright colors, ceaseless motion, and flashing skates. Suddenly the whole party came to a standstill, all talking at once to a pretty little maiden, whom they had drawn from the tide of people flowing toward the town.

"Oh, Katrinka!" they cried, in a breath, "have you heard of it? The race — we want you to join!"

"What race?" asked Katrinka, laughing.

"Why," Rychie said, "We are to have a grand skating match on the twentieth, on Mevrouw van Gleck's birthday. It's all Hilda's work. They are going to give a splendid prize to the best skater."

"Yes," chimed in half a dozen voices, "a beautiful pair of silver skates — perfectly magnificent — with such handsome black straps and shining silver bells and buckles!"

"The girls' pair is to have bells," interposed Hilda quietly, "but there is to be another pair for the boys with an arrow engraved upon the sides."

"There! I told you so!" cried nearly all the youngsters in a breath.

Katrinka looked at them with bewildered eyes. "Who is to try?" she asked.

"All of us," answered Rychie. "It will be such fun! And you must, too, Katrinka. But it's school time now, and we will talk it all over at noon. Oh! You'll join, won't you?"

Katrinka, without replying, made a graceful pirouette, and laughing out a coquettish, "Don't you hear the last bell? Catch me!" — darted off toward the schoolhouse.

All started racing, pell-mell, at this challenge, but they tried in vain to catch the bright-eyed, laughing Katrinka.

3. Hans and Gretel Find a Friend

AT NOON, the boys and girls poured forth from the schoolhouse, intent upon having an hour's practicing upon the canal.

They had skated only a few minutes when Carl Schummel said mockingly to Hilda:

"There's a pretty pair just coming on the ice! The little ragpickers! Their skates must have been a present from the king direct."

"They are patient creatures," said Hilda gently. "It must have been hard to learn to skate on such queer affairs. They are very poor peasants, you see. The boy has probably made the skates himself."

Carl was somewhat abashed.

"Patient they may be, but as for skating, they start off pretty well only to finish with a jerk. They could move well to your new staccato piece, I think."

Hilda laughed pleasantly and left him. After joining a small detachment of the racers, and sailing past every one of them, she halted beside Gretel, who with eager eyes had been watching the sport.

"What is your name, little girl?"

"Gretel, my lady," answered the child, somewhat awed by Hilda's rank, though they were nearly of the same age, "and my brother is called Hans."

"Hans is a stout fellow," said Hilda cheerily, "and seems to have a warm stove somewhere within him, but you look cold. You should wear more clothing, little one."

Gretel, who had nothing else to wear, tried to laugh as she answered:

"I am not so very little. I am almost twelve."

"Oh, I beg your pardon. You see I am nearly fourteen, and so large for my age that other girls seem small to me, but that is nothing. Perhaps you will shoot up far above me yet — not unless you dress more warmly, though."

Hans flushed as he saw tears rising in Gretel's eyes.

"My sister has not complained of the cold; but this is bitter weather, they say" — he looked sadly at Gretel.

"It is nothing," said Gretel. "I am often warm — too warm when I am skating. You are good, juffrouw, to think of it."

"No, no," answered Hilda, quite angry at herself. "I am careless, but I meant no harm. I wanted to ask you — I mean — if —" and here Hilda, coming to the point of her errand, faltered before the poorly clad children she wished to help.

"What is it, young lady?" exclaimed Hans eagerly. "If there is any service I can do, any —"

"Oh no, no," laughed Hilda, shaking off her embarrassment. "I only wished to speak to you about the grand race. Why do you not join it? You both can skate well, and the ranks are free. Anyone may enter for the prize."

Gretel looked wistfully at Hans, who answered respectfully:

"Ah, juffrouw, even if we could enter, we could skate only a few strokes with the rest. Our skates are hard wood, you see. They soon become damp, and then they stick and trip us."

Gretel said timidly, "Oh no, we can't join; but may we be there, my lady, on the great day to look on?"

"Certainly," answered Hilda, looking kindly into the two earnest faces and wishing from her heart that she had not spent so much of her monthly allowance. She had only eight kwartjes[1] left; they would buy but one pair of skates.

Looking down with a sigh at the two pairs of feet so very different in size, she asked:

"Which of you is the better skater?"

"Gretel," replied Hans promptly.

"Hans," answered Gretel, in the same breath.

Hilda smiled.

"I cannot buy you each a pair of skates, or even one good pair; but here are eight kwartjes. Decide between you which stands the best chance of winning

---

[1] A kwartje is now equal to 25 Dutch cents.

the race, and buy the skates accordingly. I wish I had enough to buy better ones — good-bye." And with a nod and a smile, Hilda, after handing the money to the electrified Hans, glided swiftly away to rejoin her companions.

"Juffrouw! Juffrouw van Gleck!" called Hans in a loud tone, skating toward her.

Hilda turned, with one hand raised to shield her eyes from the sun.

"We cannot take this money, panted Hans, "though we know your goodness in giving it."

"Why not indeed?" asked Hilda, flushing.

"Because we have not earned it."

Hilda was quick-witted. She had noticed a pretty wooden chain upon Gretel's neck.

"Carve me a chain like the one your sister wears."

"That I will, lady, with all my heart. We have whitewood in the house, fine as ivory. You shall have one tomorrow," and Hans tried to return the money.

"No, no," said Hilda decidedly. "That sum will be but a poor price for the chain," and off she darted, outstripping the fleetest among the skaters.

Hans sent a long, bewildered gaze after her; it was useless, he felt, to make any further resistance.

"It is right," he muttered, half to himself, half to his faithful shadow, Gretel. "I must work hard every minute and sit up half the night, if the mother will let me burn a candle; but the chain shall be finished. We may keep the money, Gretel."

"What a good little lady!" cried Gretel, clapping her hands with delight. "Oh Hans, was it for nothing the stork settled on our roof last summer? Do you remember how Mother said it would bring us luck, and how she cried when Janzoon Kolp shot him? And she said it would bring him trouble? But the luck has come to us at last! Now, Hans, if the mother sends us to town tomorrow you can buy the skates in the market place."

Hans shook his head. "The young lady would have given us the money to buy skates, but if I *earn* it, Gretel, it shall be spent for wool. You must have a warm jacket."

"Oh, Hans!" cried Gretel, in real dismay. "Don't say you won't buy the skates! It makes me feel just like crying — besides, I want to be cold — I mean I'm real awful warm — so now!"

Hans looked up hurriedly. He had a true Dutch horror of tears, or emotion of any kind, and most of all, he dreaded to see his sister's blue eyes overflowing.

"Now mind," cried Gretel, seeing her advantage, "I'll feel awful if you give up the skates. I don't want them. I'm not such a stingy as that; but I want *you* to have them, and then when I get bigger they'll do for me — oh-h — count the pieces, Hans. Did you ever see so many!"

Hans turned the money thoughtfully in his palm. Never in all his life had he longed so intensely for a pair of skates, for he had known of the race and fairly ached for a chance to test his powers with the others. He felt confident that with a good pair of steel runners he could readily outdistance most of the boys on the canal. On the other hand, he knew that Gretel, with her strong but lithe little frame, needed but a week's practice on good runners to make her a better skater than Rychie Korbes or even Katrinka Flack. As soon as this last thought flashed upon him, his resolve was made. If Gretel would not have the jacket, she should have the skates.

"No, Gretel," he answered at last, "I can wait. Someday I may have money enough saved to buy a fine pair. You shall have these."

Gretel's eyes sparkled; but in another instant she insisted, rather faintly:

"The young lady gave the money to *you*, Hans. I'd be real bad to take it."

Hans shook his head resolutely. By this time they had taken off their wooden "rockers" and were hastening home to tell their mother the good news.

"Hans! Gretel!" called out a familiar voice.

"Coming, Mother!" and they hastened toward the cottage, Hans still shaking the silver pieces in his hand.

On the following day, there was not a prouder nor a happier boy in all Holland than Hans Brinker, as he watched his sister flying in and out among the skaters who at sundown thronged the canal. A warm jacket had been given her by the kind-hearted Hilda, and her worn-out shoes had been cobbled into decency by Dame Brinker. As Gretel darted backward and forward, flushed with enjoyment, and quite unconscious of the many wondering glances bent upon her, she felt the smooth runners beneath her feet, and "Hans, good, good Hans!" echoed over and over in her grateful heart.

"By den donder!" exclaimed Peter van Holp to Carl Schummel, "but that little one in the red jacket and patched petticoat skates well. Just look at her! It will be a joke if she gets in the race and beats Katrinka Flack, after all."

"Hush! not so loud!" returned Carl, sneeringly. "That little lady in rags is the special pet of Hilda van Gleck. Those shining skates are her gift, if I make no mistake."

"So! so!" exclaimed Peter, with a radiant smile, for Hilda was his best friend. "She has been at her good work again!" And after cutting a double figure eight in the ice, Peter glided over to Hilda.

Hand in hand, they skated together, laughing at first, then talking in a low tone.

Strange to say, Peter van Holp soon arrived at a sudden conviction that his little sister needed a wooden chain just like Hilda's.

Two days afterward, on Saint Nicholas' Eve, Hans, having burned three candle ends and cut his thumb into the bargain, stood in the market place at Amsterdam, buying another pair of skates.

4. Shadows in the Home

GOOD DAME BRINKER! As soon as the scanty dinner
had been cleared away that noon, she had arrayed
herself in holiday attire, in honor of Saint Nicholas.
"It will brighten the children," she thought to herself, and she was not mistaken. This festival dress
had been worn very seldom during the past ten years;
before that time it had flourished at many a dance,
when she was known, far and wide, as the pretty
Meitje Klenck. The children had sometimes been
granted glimpses of it as it lay in the old oaken chest.

Even though the costume was now faded and
threadbare, it seemed gorgeous in their eyes — the
white linen tucker, the trim bodice of blue homespun,
and the reddish-brown skirt bordered with black.
The knitted woolen mitts and the dainty cap show-
ing her hair, which generally was hidden, made their
mother seem almost like a princess. Gretel fairly
danced around her mother, saying, "Oh, Mother,
how pretty you are! Look, Hans! isn't she just like a
picture?"

"Just like a picture," assented Hans cheerfully, "*just* like a picture — only I don't like those stocking things on the hands."

"Not like the mitts! Why they're very important — see — they cover up all the red. Oh, Mother, how white your arm is where the mitt leaves off — whiter than mine, oh, ever so much whiter. I declare, Mother, the bodice is tight for you. You're growing! You're surely growing!"

Dame Brinker laughed.

"This was made long ago, lovey, when I wasn't much thicker about the waist than a churn dasher. And how do you like the cap?" She turned her head from side to side.

"Oh, *ever* so much, Mother. It's b-e-a-u-tiful! See, the father is looking!"

Was the father looking? Alas, only with a dull stare. His vrouw turned toward him with a start, something like a blush rising to her cheeks, a questioning sparkle in her eye. The bright look died away in an instant.

"No, no," she sighed, "he sees nothing. Come, Hans, don't stand gaping at me all day, and the new skates waiting for you at Amsterdam."

"Ah, Mother," he answered, "you need many things. Why should I buy skates?"

"Nonsense, child. The money was given to you on purpose, or the work was — it's all the same thing. Go while the sun is high."

"Yes, and hurry back, Hans!" laughed Gretel. "We'll race on the canal tonight, if the mother lets us."

At the very threshold Hans turned to say, "Your spinning wheel wants a new treadle, Mother."

"You can make it."

"So I can. That will take no money. But you need wool and meal, and —"

"There, there! That will do. Your silver cannot buy everything. Ah! Hans, if our stolen money would but come back on this bright Saint Nicholas' Eve, how glad we would be! Only last night I prayed to the good saint himself."

"And what did you ask for, Mother?"

"Why, never to give the thieves a wink of sleep till they brought back the money, or else to brighten our wits that we might find it ourselves. Not a sight have I had of it since the day before the father was hurt — as you well know, Hans."

"That I do, Mother," he answered sadly, "though you have almost pulled down the cottage in searching."

"Aye; but it was of no use," moaned the dame. "'Hiders make best finders.'"

Hans started. "Do you think the father could tell aught?" he asked mysteriously.

"Aye, indeed," said Dame Brinker, nodding her head, "I think so, but then . . . Mayhap the father paid it off for the great silver watch we have been guarding since that day. But, no — I'll never believe it."

"The watch was not worth a quarter of the money, Mother."

"No, indeed; and your father was a shrewd man up to the last moment. He was too steady and thrifty for silly doings."

"Where *did* the watch come from, I wonder," muttered Hans, half to himself.

Dame Brinker shook her head, and looked sadly toward her husband, who sat staring blankly at the floor. Gretel stood near him, knitting.

"That we shall never know, Hans. I have shown it to the father many a time, but he does not know it from a potato. When he came in that dreadful night to supper, he handed the watch to me and told me to take good care of it until he asked for it again. Just as he opened his lips to say more, Broom Klatterboost came flying in with word that the dyke was in danger. Ah! the waters were terrible that holy Pinxter week! My man, alack, caught up his tools and ran out. That was the last I ever saw of him in his right mind. He was brought in at midnight, nearly dead, with his poor head all bruised and cut. The fever passed off in time, but never the dullness — *that* grew worse every day. We shall never know."

Hans had heard all this before. More than once he had seen his mother, in hours of sore need, take the watch from its hiding place, half resolved to sell it, but she had always conquered the temptation.

"No, Hans," she would say, "we must be nearer

starving than this before we turn faithless to the father!"

A memory of some such scene crossed her son's mind now, for after giving a heavy sigh, and filliping a crumb of wax at Gretel across the table, he said:

"Aye, Mother, you have done bravely to keep it — many a one would have tossed it off for gold long ago."

"And more shame for them!" exclaimed the dame indignantly. "*I* would not do it. Besides, the gentry are so hard on us poor folks that if they saw such a thing in our hands, even if we told all, they might suspect the father of —"

Hans flushed angrily.

"They would not *dare* to say such a thing, Mother! If they did — I'd —"

He clenched his fist, and seemed to think that the rest of his sentence was too terrible to utter in her presence.

Dame Brinker smiled proudly through her tears at this interruption.

"Ah, Hans, thou'rt a true, brave lad. We will never part company with the watch. In his dying hour the dear father might wake and ask for it."

"Might *wake*, Mother?" echoed Hans, "wake — and know us?"

"Aye, child," almost whispered his mother, "such things have been."

By this time Hans had nearly forgotten his proposed errand to Amsterdam. His mother had seldom spoken so familiarly with him. He felt himself now to be not only her son, but her friend, her adviser.

"You are right, Mother. We must never give up the watch. For the father's sake, we will guard it always. The money, though, may come to light when we least expect it."

"Never!" cried Dame Brinker, taking the last stitch from her needle with a jerk and laying the unfinished knitting heavily upon her lap. "There is no chance! One thousand guilders[1] — all gone in a day! One thousand guilders. Oh! what ever *did* become of them? If they went in an evil way, the thief would have confessed by now on his dying bed — he would not dare to die with such a guilt on his soul!"

"He may not be dead yet," said Hans soothingly. "Any day we may hear of him."

"Ah, child," she said in a changed tone, "what thief would ever come *here?* It was always neat and clean, thank God! but not fine; for the father and I saved and saved that we might have something laid by. 'Little and often soon fills the pouch.'

"We found it so, in truth; besides, the father had a goodly sum already, for service done to the Heerhocht lands at the time of the great inundation. Every week we had a guilder left over, sometimes more; for the father worked extra hours, and could

---

[1] A guilder, or *gulden,* is now worth 100 Dutch cents or about 28 American cents.

get high pay for his labor. Every Saturday night we put something by, except the time when you had the fever, Hans, and when Gretel came. At last the pouch grew so full that I mended an old stocking and commenced again. There was great pay in those days if a man was quick at engineer work.

"Sometimes, at supper, the father and I would talk about a new chimney and good winter room for the cow; but my man forsooth had finer plans even than that. 'A big sail,' he'd say, 'catches the wind — we can do what we will soon.' Every week he would take out the stocking and drop in the money, and laugh and kiss me as we tied it up together.

"Up with you, Hans! There you sit gaping, and the day awasting!" added Dame Brinker tartly, blushing to find that she had been speaking too freely to her boy. "It's high time you were on your way."

Hans had seated himself and was looking earnestly into her face. He arose and, in almost a whisper, asked:

"Have you ever *tried*, Mother?"

She understood him.

"Yes, child, often. But the father only laughs, or he stares at me so strange I am glad to ask no more. When you and Gretel had the fever last winter, and our bread was nearly gone, and I could earn nothing for fear you would die while my face was turned, oh! I tried then! I smoothed his hair, and whispered to him soft as a kitten about the money — where it

was — who had it. Alack! He would pick at my sleeve
and whisper gibberish till my blood ran cold. At last,
while Gretel lay whiter than snow, and you were
raving on the bed, I screamed to him — it seemed as
if he *must* hear me — 'Raff, where is our money? Do
you know aught of the money, Raff? — the money in
the pouch and the stocking, in the big chest?' But
I might as well have talked to a stone — I might
as — "

The mother's voice sounded so strange, and her
eye was so bright, that Hans, with a new anxiety,
laid his hand upon her shoulder.

"Come, Mother," he said, "let us try to forget this
money. I am big and strong, and Gretel is very quick.
Soon all will be prosperous with us again. Why,
Mother, Gretel and I would rather see thee bright
and happy than to have all the silver in the world —
wouldn't we, Gretel?"

"Mother knows it," said Gretel, sobbing.

Dame Brinker was startled at her children's emotion; glad, too, for it proved how loving and true
they were.

"Hoity-toity! Pretty talk we're having, and Saint
Nicholas' Eve almost here! Three turns of the needle
will finish this toe, and then you may have as good a
pair of hose as ever were knitted to sell to the hosier
in Amsterdam. That will give us three quarter-
guilders if you make good trade, and you may buy

four waffles. We'll keep the Feast of Saint Nicholas after all."

Gretel clapped her hands. "That will be fine! Annie Bouman told me what grand times they will have in the big houses tonight. But we will be merry, too. Hans will have beautiful new skates — and then there'll be the waffles! Oh-h! Don't break them, brother Hans. Wrap them well, and button them under your jacket very carefully."

"Certainly," replied Hans, quite gruff with pleasure and importance. He kissed his mother's plump cheek, rosy and fresh yet, in spite of all her troubles.

"My mother is the best in the world, and I would be right glad to have a pair of skates, but" — as he buttoned his jacket he looked in a troubled way toward a strange figure crouching by the hearthstone — "if my money would bring a doctor from Amsterdam to see the father, something might yet be done."

"A doctor would not come, Hans, for twice that money, and it would do no good if he did. Ah! how many guilders I once spent for that; but the dear, good father would not waken. It is God's will. Go, Hans, and buy the skates."

5. Hans Has His Way

THE BRINKERS lived near the village of Broek, with its quiet, spotless streets, its frozen rivulets, its yellow brick pavements and bright wooden houses. It was a village where neatness and show were in full bloom, but the inhabitants seemed to be either asleep or dead. Not a footprint marred the sanded paths, where pebbles and sea shells lay in fanciful designs. Every window shutter was closed tightly.

Hans glanced toward the houses as he shook his silver kwartjes, and wondered whether it were really true, as he had often heard, that some of the people of Broek were so rich they used kitchen utensils of solid gold.

He had seen Mevrouw van Stoop's sweet cheeses in market, and he knew that the lofty dame earned many a bright silver guilder in selling them. But did she set the cream to rise in golden pans? Did she use a golden skimmer?

These thoughts ran through his mind as he turned his face toward Amsterdam, not five miles away. The ice on the canal was perfect; but his wooden runners, so soon to be cast aside, squeaked a dismal farewell as he scraped and skimmed along.

Suddenly, whom should he see skating toward him but the great Dr. Boekman, the most famous physician and surgeon in Holland. Hans had never met him before, but he had seen his engraved likeness in many of the shop windows of Amsterdam. It was a face that one could never forget. Thin and lank, with stern blue eyes and tightly compressed lips, he certainly was not a very jolly or sociable-looking person, nor one that a well-trained boy would care to approach unbidden.

But Hans *was* bidden, and that too by a voice he seldom disregarded: his own conscience.

"Here comes the greatest doctor in the world," whispered the voice. "God has sent him; you have no right to buy skates when you might, with the same money, purchase such aid for your father!"

The wooden runners gave an exultant squeak. Hundreds of beautiful skates seemed to gleam and vanish in the air above Hans. He felt the money tingle in his fingers. The old doctor looked fearfully grim and forbidding. Hans's heart was in his throat, but he found voice enough to cry out, just as he was passing:

"Mynheer Boekman!"

The great man halted, and sticking out his thin
underlip, looked scowlingly about him.

Hans was in for it now.

"Mynheer," he panted, drawing close to the fierce-
looking doctor, "I knew you could be no other than
the famous Dr. Boekman. I have to ask a great favor —"

"Humph!" muttered the doctor, preparing to skate
past the intruder. "Get out of the way — I've no
money — never give to beggars."

"I am no beggar, mynheer," retorted Hans proudly,
at the same time producing his mite of silver with a
grand air. "I wish to consult with you about my
father. He is a living man, but sits like one dead. He
cannot think. His words mean nothing — but he is not
sick. He fell on the dykes."

"Hey? what?" cried the doctor, beginning to listen.

Hans told the whole story in an incoherent way,
dashing off a tear once or twice as he talked, and
finally ending with an earnest —

"Oh, do see him, mynheer. His body is well — it is
only his mind. I know this money is not enough; but
take it, mynheer, I will earn more — I know I will. Oh!
I will work for you all my life if only you will cure my
father!"

What was the matter with the old doctor? A bright-
ness like sunlight beamed from his face. His eyes
were kind and moist; the hand that had lately
clutched his cane, as if to strike, was laid gently upon
Hans's shoulder.

"Put up your money, boy. I do not want it — we will see your father. It is a hopeless case, I fear. How long did you say?"

"Ten years, mynheer," Hans cried, radiant with sudden hope.

"Ah! a bad case; but I shall see him. Let me think. Today I start for Leyden, to return in a week; then you may expect me. Where is it?"

"A mile south of Broek, mynheer, near the canal. It is only a poor hut. Any of the children thereabout can point it out to your honor," added Hans, with a heavy sigh. "They are all half afraid of the place; they call it the idiot's cottage."

"That will do," said the doctor, hurrying on with a bright backward nod at Hans. "I shall be there. A hopeless case," he muttered to himself, "but the boy pleases me. His eye is like my poor Laurens'. Confound it, shall I never forget that young scoundrel!" And scowling more darkly than ever, the doctor pursued his silent way.

Again Hans was skating toward Amsterdam on the squeaking wooden runners; again his fingers tingled against the money in his pocket; again the boyish whistle rose unconsciously to his lips.

"Shall I hurry home," he was thinking, "to tell the good news, or shall I get the waffles and the new skates first? Whew! I think I'll go on!"

And so Hans bought the skates.

6. Introducing Jacob Poot
and His Cousin

Hans AND GRETEL had a fine frolic early on that Saint Nicholas' Eve. There was a bright moon; and their mother, though she believed herself to be without any hope of her husband's improvement, had been made so happy at the prospect of the doctor's visit that she had yielded to the children's entreaties for an hour's skating before bedtime.

Hans was delighted with his new skates, and in his eagerness to show Gretel how perfectly they "worked" did many things upon the ice that caused her to exclaim and clasp her hands in solemn admiration. They were not alone, although they seemed to be unnoticed by the other groups there.

The two van Holps and Carl Schummel were there, testing their fleetness. Out of four trials Peter van Holp had beaten three times. Consequently Carl, never very amiable, was in anything but a good humor. A new thought seized Carl, or rather he seized on a thought and assaulted his friends with it.

"I say, boys, let's put a stop to those young rag-pickers from the idiot's cottage joining the race. Hilda must be crazy to think of it. Katrinka Flack and Rychie Korbes are furious at the very idea of racing with the girl, and for my part I don't blame them. As for the boy, if we've a spark of manhood in us we will scorn the very idea of —"

"Certainly we will!" interposed Peter van Holp, purposely mistaking Carl's meaning, "who doubts it? No fellow with a spark of manhood in him would refuse to let in two good skaters just because they were poor!"

Carl wheeled about savagely:

"Not so fast, master! And I'd thank you not to put words in other people's mouths. You'd best not try it again."

Just then his friend, Jacob Poot, was seen approaching. They could not distinguish his features at first; but as he was the stoutest boy in the neighborhood, there could be no mistaking his form.

"Halloo, here comes Fatty!" exclaimed Carl. "There's someone with him — a slender fellow, a stranger."

"That's Jacob's English cousin," put in Master Voost, delighted at being able to give the information. "He's got such a funny little name: Ben Dobbs. He's going to stay with Jacob until after the grand race."

The boys halted, bracing themselves against the frosty air as Jacob Poot and his friend drew near.

"This is my cousin, boys," said Jacob, rather out
of breath — "Benjamin Dobbs. He's a 'John Bull,' and
he's going to be in the race."

All crowded about the newcomers. Benjamin soon
made up his mind that the Hollanders were a fine set
of fellows, but at first he felt decidedly awkward
among his cousin's friends. Though most of them had
studied English and French, they were shy about at-
tempting to speak either, and he made very funny
blunders when he tried to speak in Dutch.

However, the fun of skating glides over all barriers of speech. Ben soon felt that he knew the boys
well; and when Jacob (with a sprinkling of French
and English for Ben's benefit) told of a grand project
they had planned, his cousin could now and then put
in a "Ya," or a nod, in quite a familiar way.

The project *was* a grand one, and there was to be
a fine opportunity for carrying it out; for this year,
besides the allotted holiday for the Festival of Saint
Nicholas, four extra days' vacation were to be allowed.

Jacob and Ben had obtained permission to go on a
long skating journey — from Broek to The Hague, the
capital of Holland, a distance of nearly fifty miles.

"And now, boys," added Jacob, when he had told
the plan, "who will go with us?"

"I will! I will!" cried the boys eagerly.

"We can stop at Haarlem, Jacob, so your cousin can
hear the great organ at St. Bavon's," said Peter van
Holp eagerly, "and at Leyden, too, where there's no

end to the sights; and spend a day and night at The Hague. My married sister, who lives there, will be delighted to see us, and the next morning we can start for home."

"All right!" responded Jacob, who was not much of a talker.

Peter van Holp took out a bulgy gold watch and, holding it toward the moonlight as well as his benumbed fingers would permit, called out:

"Halloo! it's nearly eight o'clock! Saint Nicholas is about by this time, and I for one want to see the little ones stare. Good night!"

"Good night!" cried one and all, and off they started, shouting, singing, and laughing as they flew along.

Where were Gretel and Hans?

They had skated about an hour, keeping aloof from the others, quite content with each other's company, and Gretel had exclaimed, "Oh, Hans, how beautiful! how fine! to think that we both have skates! I tell you the stork brought us good luck!" — when they heard something!

It was a scream — a very faint scream. No one else upon the canal observed it, but Hans knew its meaning too well. Gretel saw him turn white in the moonlight as he hastily tore off his skates.

"The father!" he cried. "He has frightened our mother!" and Gretel ran after him toward the house as rapidly as she could.

7. The Festival of Saint Nicholas

We all know how, before the Christmas tree came to our country, a certain "jolly old elf," with "eight tiny reindeer," used to drive his sleighload of toys up to our housetops, and then bound down the chimney to fill the stockings so hopefully hung by the fireplace. His friends called him Santa Claus.

In Holland, Saint Nicholas is a veritable saint, and often appears in full costume, with his embroidered robes glittering with gems and gold, his miter, his crosier, and his jeweled gloves. *Here*, Santa Claus comes rollicking along on the twenty-fourth of December, our Christmas Eve. But in Holland, Saint Nicholas visits earth on December fifth, a time especially appropriated to him. Very early in the morning of the sixth, he distributes his candies, toys, and treasures; then vanishes for a year.

On Saint Nicholas Eve, in the great houses, the families gather in the grand parlor to await the arrival of the saint. The children, all merry and eager and excited, play games and sing. At last there is a knock on the door.

"Come in," calls the mother.

The door slowly opens, and there stands the Saint Nicholas! Almost like a father he addresses each child by name, reproving and praising him for his behavior in the past year. At last he says:

"With one and all I avow myself well content. Therefore, my blessing upon you all. Tomorrow you shall find more substantial proofs that I have been in your midst. Farewell!"

With these words there is a great shower of sugarplums on a linen sheet spread out in front of the parlor doors. A general scramble follows, and the children fairly tumble over each other in their eagerness to fill their baskets.

Then the bravest of the youngsters springs up and bursts open the closed doors — in vain they peer into the mysterious room — Saint Nicholas is nowhere to be seen.

Soon there is a general rush to another room, where stands a table covered with fine white linen damask. Each child, in a flutter of excitement, places a shoe on it. The door is then carefully locked, and its key is hidden in the mother's bedroom. Next follow goodnight kisses, a grand family procession to the upper floor, merry farewells at bedroom doors — and silence reigns at last.

Early the next morning the door is solemnly unlocked and opened in the presence of the assembled household, and lo! the sight they behold proves Saint Nicholas to be a saint of his word!

Every shoe is filled to overflowing, and beside each shoe stands many a bright-colored pile. The table is heavy with its load of presents — candies, toys, trinkets, books, and other articles. Everyone has gifts, from grandfather down to the baby.

Carl Schummel was quite busy at his house during the next day, assuring little children, confidentially, that not Saint Nicholas, but their own fathers and mothers had produced the oracle and loaded the tables. But *we* know better than that.

And yet if this were a saint's doing, why had he not visited the Brinker cottage? Why was that one home, so dark and sorrowful, passed by?

8. What the Boys Saw
and Did in Amsterdam

"ARE WE ALL HERE?" cried Peter, in high glee, as the party assembled upon the canal early the next morning, equipped for their skating journey. "Let me see. As Jacob has made me captain, I must call the roll. Carl Schummel — you here?"

"Ya!"

"Jacob Poot!"

"Ya!"

"Benjamin Dobbs!"

"Ya-a!"

"Lambert van Mounen!"

"Ya!"

"That's lucky! Couldn't get on without *you*, as you're the only one who can speak English. — Ludwig van Holp!"

"Ya!"

"Voostenwalbert Schimmelpenninck!"

No answer.

"Ah! the little rogue has been kept at home. Now then, it's just eight o'clock — glorious weather, and the ice is as firm as a rock — we'll be at Amsterdam in thirty minutes. One, two, three — START!"

True enough, in less than half an hour they had crossed a dyke of solid masonry and were in the very heart of the great metropolis of the Netherlands — a walled city of ninety-five islands and nearly five hundred bridges, of tall houses with their forked chimneys and gable ends facing the street, of narrow streets and canals everywhere crossing the city.

The city was in full festival array. Every shop was gorgeous in honor of Saint Nicholas. Captain Peter was forced, more than once, to order his men away from the tempting show windows. Everything in the way of toys was displayed — intricate mechanical toys, mimic fishing boats, like the queer craft Ben had seen about Rotterdam, and tiny canalboats, fitted out complete. Ben longed to buy one for his brother Robby in England, but he had no money to spare; the party had agreed to take with them merely the sum required for each boy's expenses, and to give the purse to Peter for safekeeping. So Ben devoted his energies to sight-seeing.

The boys enjoyed hasty glimpses of the four principal avenues of Amsterdam. A canal runs through the center of each, with a well-paved road on either side, lined with stately buildings. Then Peter called out:

"Skates off! There's the museum!"

It was open, and there was no charge on that day for admission. In they went, shuffling, to hear the sound of their shoes on the polished floor.

In the huge Rijksmuseum are some of the finest and rarest paintings by Dutch masters to be seen anywhere — very old ones painted on wood, and many by the great Amsterdam painter, Rembrandt.

Ben noticed a small picture by Gerard Dou, called "Evening School," that seemed to be lit through its own windows.

"Hey!" called Lambert, in a loud whisper, "come look at this 'Bear Hunt.'"

It was a fine painting by Paul Potter, a Dutch artist who had produced excellent paintings before he was sixteen years old. The boys admired it because the subject pleased them. They passed carelessly by small masterpieces of Vermeer and van Ruysdael, and stared at an ugly picture by van der Venne, representing a sea fight between the Dutch and English.

"Come on, fellows!" cried Peter at last. "Ten o'clock. Time we were off!"

They hastened to the canal.

"Skates on! Are you ready? One, two — halloo! where's Poot?"

Sure enough where *was* Poot?

A square opening had just been cut in the ice not ten yards off. Peter observed it, and without a word skated rapidly toward it. All the others followed, of course.

Peter looked in. They all looked in, then stared anxiously at each other.

"Poot!" screamed Peter, peering into the hole again. All was still. The black water gave no sign; it was already glazing on top.

Van Mounen turned mysteriously to Ben.

"Didn't he have a fit once?"

"My goodness, yes!" answered Ben, in a great fright.

"Then, depend upon it, he's been taken with one in the museum!"

The boys caught his meaning. Every skate was off in a twinkling, and off they scampered to the rescue.

They did indeed find Jacob — fast asleep! There he lay in a recess of the gallery, snoring like a trooper! The chorus of laughter that followed this discovery brought an angry official to the spot.

"What now! None of this racket! Here, you beer barrel, wake up!" and Jacob received a very unceremonious shaking.

As soon as Peter saw that Jacob's condition was not serious, he hastened to the street, while the rest of the boys came down, dragging the bewildered and indignant Jacob in their midst.

Time to start again. Jacob was wide awake at last. The ice was a little rough and broken just there, but every boy was in high spirits.

Skating along at full speed, they heard the train from Amsterdam coming close behind them.

"Halloo!" cried Ludwig, glancing toward the rail-

road track. "Who can't beat a locomotive? Let's give
it a race!"

For an instant the boys were ahead — only for an
instant, but even *that* was something.

This excitement over, they began to travel more
leisurely. Sometimes they stopped to exchange a word
with the guards who were stationed along the canal.
These men, in winter, attend to keeping the surface
of the ice cleared off.

Now and then the boys clambered among the ice-
bound canalboats crowded together in a widened
harbor off the canal, but the watchful guards would
soon order them down.

Nothing could be straighter than the canal upon
which our party were skating, and nothing straighter
than the long rows of willow trees that stood, bare
and wispy, along the bank. On the opposite side,
lifted high above the surrounding country, lay the
carriage road on top of the great dyke built to keep
the Haarlem Lake within bounds. Stretching out far
in the distance, until it became lost in a point, was
the glassy canal with its many skaters, its brown-
winged iceboats and pushchairs.

"How very different you are from the Poots!" exclaimed Lambert suddenly to Ben, as they skated
along side by side.

"We *are* cousins, but the relationship is not very
close. I like Jacob awfully well, though. He is the
truest-hearted, best-natured boy I ever knew. I sup-

pose my sister Jenny would open her eyes at some of Aunt Poot's ways. Aunt is so different from Mother, and her house too — everything is different."

"Of course," assented Lambert complacently. "I saw much to admire in England, and I hope I shall be sent back with you to study at Oxford; but taking everything together, I like Holland best."

"Of course you do," said Ben, in a tone of hearty approval. "Nothing like loving one's own country. It is strange, though, to have such a warm feeling for such a cold place. If we were not exercising all the time we should freeze outright."

Lambert laughed.

"That's your English blood, Benjamin. *I'm* not cold. Halloo! Captain van Holp," Lambert called out in Dutch, "what do you say to stopping at yonder farmhouse and warming our toes?"

"Who is cold?" asked Peter, turning around.

"Benjamin Dobbs."

"Benjamin Dobbs shall be warmed," and the party was brought to a halt.

9. Haarlem

THE FARMHOUSE looked most inviting, with its low roof of bright red tiles. In answer to Peter's subdued knock, a fair-haired, rosy-cheeked lass in holiday attire opened the upper half of the door, which was divided across the middle, and inquired their errand.

"May we enter and warm ourselves, juffrouw?" asked the captain respectfully.

"Yes, and welcome," was the reply, as the lower half of the door swung open. Every boy before entering rubbed his feet on the rough mat, and each made his best bow.

The rosy-cheeked maiden bustled about, giving the boys polished high-backed chairs to sit upon, making the fire blaze up, and bringing forth a great square of gingerbread and a stone jug of sour wine. She laughed and nodded at the boys, who ate like hungry wolves. She pulled off Jacob's mitten, which was torn at the thumb, and mended it, biting off the thread with her white teeth and saying, "Now it will be warmer." Finally she shook hands with every boy in turn, and insisted upon filling their pockets with gingerbread!

When the boys were fairly on their way again, they came in sight of Zwanenburg Castle with its massive stone front, and its gateway towers, each surmounted with a sculptured swan.

"Halfway, boys," said Peter, "off with your skates."

"You see," explained Lambert to his companion, "the Y arm of the Zuider Zee and the Haarlem Lake meeting here make it rather troublesome. The river is five feet higher than the land, so the dykes and sluice gates must be extra strong. The spring water of the lake, they say, has the most wonderful bleaching powers. The castle's a big affair, isn't it?"

"Yes. What do those swans mean? Anything?" asked Ben, looking up at the stone gate towers.

"The swan is held almost in reverence by us Hollanders. These give the building its name, Zwanenburg — Swan Castle. It was once the residence of Christiaan Brünings."

"What about *him*?" asked Ben.

"Peter could answer you better than I," said Lambert. "But I have often heard my grandfather speak of Brünings. He was a great engineer. There's no counting the improvements he made in dykes and sluices and water mills, and all that kind of thing. We Hollanders, you know, consider our great engineers as the highest of public benefactors. He died years ago, and there's a monument to his memory in the Cathedral of Haarlem."

It was nearly one o'clock when Captain Peter and his company entered the grand old city of Haarlem. They had skated nearly seventeen miles since morning, but were still as fresh as young eagles.

"Come on! It's nearly lunchtime," Peter said, as they neared a coffeehouse on the main street. "We must have something more solid than the pretty maid's gingerbread" — and the captain plunged his hands into his pockets as if to say, "There's money enough here to feed an army!"

"Halloo!" cried Lambert. "What ails the man?"

Peter, pale and staring, was clapping his hands against his chest and sides.

"He's sick!" cried Ben.

"No, he's lost something," said Carl.

Peter could only gasp, "The pocketbook, with all our money in it — it's gone!"

For an instant all were too much startled to speak.

Carl at last came out with a gruff, "No sense in letting one fellow have all the money. I said so from the first. Look in your other pocket."

"I did — it isn't there."

"Open your underjacket — "

Peter obeyed mechanically. He even took off his hat and looked into it — then thrust his hand desperately into every pocket.

"It's gone, boys," he said at last, in a hopeless tone. "No lunch for us, nor dinner either. What is to be done? We can't get on without money. If we were in Amsterdam, I could get as much as we want, but there is not a man in Haarlem from whom I can borrow a stiver.[1] Doesn't one of you know anyone here who would lend us a few guilders?"

Each boy looked into five blank faces.

"That wouldn't do," Carl said crossly. "I know some people here — rich ones too — but father would flog me soundly if I borrowed a cent from anyone. He has 'An honest man need not borrow' written over the gateway of his summerhouse."

"Humph!" responded Peter, not particularly admiring the sentiment just at that moment.

The boys grew desperately hungry at once.

"It was my fault," said Jacob, in his broken English, to Ben. "I said first, all of us had better let van Holp hold the money."

"Nonsense, Jacob; you did it all for the best."

Ben said this in such a sprightly tone that the two van Holps and Carl felt sure he had proposed a plan that would relieve the party at once.

"What? what? Tell us, van Mounen," they cried.

"He says it is not Jacob's fault that the money is lost — that he did it for the best when he proposed

---

[1] A stiver, or *stuiver*, is now worth five Dutch cents.

that van Holp should put all of our money into his purse."

"Is that all?" said Ludwig dismally. "How much money have we lost?"

"Don't you remember?" said Peter. "We each put in exactly ten guilders. The purse had sixty guilders in it. I am the stupidest fellow in the world; little Schimmelpenninck would have made a better captain."

"We all know it was an accident," growled Carl, "but that doesn't help matters. We must have money, van Holp — even if we have to sell your wonderful watch."

"Sell my mother's birthday present! Never! I will sell my coat, my hat, anything but my watch."

"Come, come," said Jacob pleasantly, "we are making too much of this. We can go home and start again in a day or two."

"*You* may be able to get another ten-guilder piece," said Carl, "but the rest of us will not find it so easy. If we go home, we stay home, you may depend."

Peter, whose good nature had not forsaken him before, for a moment grew indignant.

"Do you think I will let you suffer for my carelessness?" he exclaimed. "I have three times sixty guilders in my strongbox at home!"

"Oh, I beg your pardon," said Carl hastily, adding in a surlier tone, "Well, I see no better way than to go back hungry."

"I see a better plan than that," said the captain.

"What is it?" cried the boys.

"Why, to make the best of a bad business and go back pleasantly, and like men," said Peter, looking so gallant as he turned his frank face and clear blue eyes upon them that they caught his spirit.

"Ho for Peter!" they shouted.

"We may as well make up our minds there's no place like Broek, after all — and that we mean to be there in two hours. Is that agreed to?"

"Agreed!" cried all, as they ran to the canal.

"On with your skates! Are you ready? Now. One, two, three, start!"

And the boyish faces that left Haarlem at that signal were nearly as bright as those that had entered it half an hour before.

10. Hans

"Donder and Blixin!" cried Carl angrily, before the party had skated twenty yards from the city gates, "if here isn't that wooden-skate ragamuffin in the patched leather breeches. That fellow is everywhere, confound him! We'll be lucky," he added, in as sneering a tone as he dared to assume, "if our captain doesn't order us to halt and shake hands with him."

"Your captain is a terrible fellow," said Peter pleasantly, "but this is a false alarm, Carl — I cannot spy your bugbear anywhere among the skaters. Ah! there he is! Why, what is the matter with the lad?"

Hans' countenance brightened at once. "Ah! mynheer, is that you? It is well we meet!"

"Just like his impertinence," hissed Carl Schummel, darting scornfully past his companions.

"I am glad to see you, Hans," responded Peter cheerily, "but you look troubled. Can I help you?"

"I have a trouble, mynheer," answered Hans, casting down his eyes. Then lifting them again with almost a happy expression, he added, "but it is Hans

Brinker who can help Mynheer van Holp this time."

"How?" asked Peter, making in his blunt Dutch way, no attempt to conceal his surprise.

"By giving you this, mynheer "— and Hans held forth the missing purse.

"Hurrah!" shouted the boys, taking their cold hands from their pockets to wave them joyfully in the air. But Peter said, "Thank you, Hans Brinker," in a tone that made Hans feel as if the king had knelt to him.

Meantime Peter had drawn Hans aside.

"How did you know it was my purse?" he asked.

"You paid me three guilders yesterday, mynheer, for making the whitewood chain, telling me that I must buy skates."

"Yes, I remember."

"I saw your purse then; it was of yellow leather."

"And where did you find it today?"

"I left my home this morning, mynheer, in great trouble. As I skated, I took no heed until I stumbled against some lumber, and while I was rubbing my knee I saw your purse nearly hidden under a log."

"That place! Ah, I remember now — just as we were passing it I pulled my scarf from my pocket, and probably puiled out the purse at the same time. It would have been gone but for you, Hans. Here" — pouring out the contents — "you must give us the pleasure of dividing the money with you."

"No, mynheer," answered Hans. He spoke quietly, without pretense or any grace of manner, but Peter felt rebuked somehow and put the silver back.

"I like that boy," he thought to himself, then added aloud, "May I ask about this trouble of yours, Hans?"

"Ah, mynheer, it is a sad case — but I have waited here too long. I am going to Leyden to see the great Dr. Boekman."

"Dr. Boekman!" exclaimed Peter in astonishment.

"Yes, mynheer, and I have not a moment to lose. Good day!"

"Stay, I am going that way. Come, my lads! Shall we return to Haarlem?"

"Yes," cried the boys eagerly — and off they started.

"Now," said Peter, drawing near Hans, both skimming the ice easily and lightly as they skated on together. "We are going to stop at Leyden, and if you are going there only with a message to Dr. Boekman, can't I do the errand for you? The boys may be too tired to skate so far today, but I will promise to see him early tomorrow if he is in the city."

"Ah, mynheer, that would be serving me indeed; it is not the distance I dread, but leaving my mother so long."

"Is she ill?"

"No, mynheer. It is the father. You may have heard about him — how he has been without wit for many a year — ever since the great Schlossen Mill was built; but his body has been well and strong. Last night the mother knelt upon the hearth to blow the peat — it is his only delight to sit and watch the live embers,

and she will blow them into a blaze every hour of the
day to please him. Before she could stir, he sprang
upon her like a giant and held her close to the fire,
all the time laughing and shaking his head.

"I was on the canal, but I heard the mother scream
and ran to her. The father had never loosened his
hold, and her gown was smoking. I tried to deaden
the fire, but with one hand he pushed me off. There
was no water in the cottage, or I could have done
better; and all that time he laughed — such a terrible
laugh, mynheer; hardly a sound, but all in his face.
I tried to pull her away, but that only made it worse.
Then — it was dreadful, but could I see the mother
burn? I beat him — beat him with a stool. He tossed
me away. The gown was on fire! I *would* put it out. I
can't remember well after that; I found myself upon
the floor and the mother was praying. It seemed to
me that she was in a blaze, and all the while I could
hear that laugh.

"My sister Gretel screamed out that he was holding
the mother close to the very coals. *I* could not tell!
Gretel flew to the closet and filled a porringer with
the food he liked and put it upon the floor. Then,
mynheer, he left the mother and crawled to it like a
little child. She was not burnt, only a part of her
clothing. Ah, how kind she was to him all night,
watching and tending him. He slept in a high fever,
with his hand pressed to his head. The mother says
he has done that so much of late, as though he felt

pain there. Ah, mynheer, I did not mean to tell you.
If the father were himself, he wouldn't harm a kitten."

For a moment the two boys moved on in silence.

"It is terrible," said Peter at last. "How is he
today?"

"Very sick, mynheer."

"Why go for Dr. Boekman, Hans? There are others
in Amsterdam who could help him, perhaps. Boekman
is a famous man, sought only by the wealthiest, and
they often wait upon him in vain."

"He promised, mynheer — he promised me yesterday to come to the father in a week. But now that the
change has come, we cannot wait. We think the poor
father is dying. Oh mynheer, you can plead with him
to come quick. He will not wait a whole week and
our father dying. The good meester is so kind."

"So *kind!* echoed Peter, in astonishment. "Why,
he is known as the crossest man in Holland!"

"He looks so because he has no fat and his head is
busy, but his heart is kind, I know. Tell the meester
what I have told you, mynheer, and he will come."

"I hope so, Hans, with all my heart. You are in
haste to turn homeward, I see. Promise me that should
you need a friend, you will go to my mother, at
Broek. Tell her I bade you see her; and, Hans Brinker,
not as a reward, but as a gift, take these guilders."

Hans shook his head resolutely.

"No, no, mynheer. I cannot take it. If I could find
work in Broek or at the South Mill I would be glad,

but it is the same story everywhere: 'Wait till spring.'"

"It is well you speak of it," said Peter eagerly, "for my father needs help at once. Your chain pleased him much. He said, 'That boy has a clean cut; he would be good at carving.' There is to be a carved portal to our new summerhouse, and father will pay well for the job."

"God is good!" cried Hans in sudden delight. "I have never tried big work, but I know I can do it."

"Well, tell my father you are the Hans Brinker of whom I spoke. He will be glad to serve you."

Hans stared in honest surprise.

"Thank you, mynheer."

"Now captain," shouted Carl, anxious to appear as good-humored as possible, by way of atonement, "here we are in the midst of Haarlem, and no word from you yet. We await your orders, and we're hungry as wolves."

Peter made a cheerful answer, and turned hurriedly to Hans. "Come, get something to eat, and I will detain you no longer."

What a quick, wistful look Hans threw upon him! Peter wondered why he had not noticed before that the poor boy was hungry.

"Ah, mynheer, even now the mother may need me, the father may be worse — I must not wait. May God care for you" — and, nodding hastily, Hans turned his face homeward and was gone.

"Come, boys," sighed Peter, "now for our lunch!"

11. Homes

THE YOUNG DUTCHMEN had by no means forgotten the great skating race which was to take place on the twentieth. Even Ben had never once, through all the sight-seeing, lost a certain vision of the silver skates. They haunted him night and day.

He never doubted that his English fleetness and strength could at any time enable him, on the ice, to put all Holland to shame. Ben certainly was a superb skater. He had not enjoyed half the opportunities for practicing that had fallen to his new comrades, but he had improved his share to the utmost; and was, besides, so strong of frame, so supple of limb, such a trim, quick, graceful fellow in every way, that he had taken to skating naturally.

Only to the heavy heart of poor Hans had the vision of the silver skates failed to appear.

Even Gretel had seen them flitting before her as she sat beside her mother through those hours of weary watching — not as prizes to be won, but as treasures passing hopelessly beyond her reach.

Rychie, Hilda, and Katrinka — why, they had scarcely known any other thought than, "The race! the race! It will come off on the twentieth!"

These three girls were friends. Though of nearly the same age, talent, and station, they were as different as girls could be.

Hilda van Gleck was a warmhearted girl of fourteen. Rychie Korbes was beautiful to look upon, far more sparkling and pretty than Hilda, but not half so bright and sunny within.

To Rychie's mind, Gretel had no right to feel, to hope. Above all, the poor should never cross the paths of their betters — that is, not in a disagreeable way. They could toil and labor for them, but nothing more. "If they suffer, don't trouble me about it," was Rychie's secret motto. And yet how witty she was, how tastefully she dressed, how charmingly she sang, how much feeling she displayed (for pet kittens and rabbits), and how completely she could bewitch sensible, honest-minded lads like Lambert van Mounen and Ludwig van Holp!

Carl was too much like her, within, to be an earnest admirer. He, being deep and surly, and always uncomfortably in earnest, of course preferred the lively Katrinka. She was a coquette in her infancy and childhood, and now a coquette in her school days. Without a thought of harm, she skipped through her studies, her duties, even her little troubles. Everyone liked her, but who could love her? She was never in earnest. A pleasant face, a pleasant heart, a pleasant manner — these only satisfy for an hour. Poor, empty Katrinka.

How different were the homes of these three girls from the tumbling old cottage where Gretel dwelt! Rychie lived in a beautiful house near Amsterdam, where the carved sideboards were laden with services of silver and gold, and where silken tapestries hung in folds from ceiling to floor.

Hilda's father owned the largest mansion in Broek. Its glittering roof of polished tiles, and its boarded front, painted in half a dozen various colors, were the admiration of the neighborhood.

Katrinka's home, not a mile distant, was the finest of Dutch country seats. The garden was stiffly laid out in little paths and patches, like a game of Chinese checkers. In summer it was beautiful, and such a tulip bed!

Carl was both right and wrong when he said that Katrinka and Rychie were furious at the very idea of Gretel joining in the race. He had heard Rychie declare it was "disgraceful, shameful, too bad!" And he had seen Katrinka nod her pretty head, and heard her sweetly echo "shameful, too bad!" That had satisfied him. He never suspected that had Hilda, not Rychie, first talked with Katrinka upon the subject, she would have said, "Certainly, let her join us," and would have skipped off thinking no more about it.

Poor little Gretel! Her home was sad and dark

enough now. Raff Brinker lay moaning upon his rough
bed, and his vrouw, forgetting and forgiving everything, bathed his forehead, his lips, weeping and
praying that he might not die. Hans, as we know, had
started in desperation for Leyden to search for Dr.
Boekman, and induce him, if possible, to come to their
father at once. Gretel, filled with a strange dread, had
done the work as well as she could, wiped the rough
brick floor, brought peat to build up the slow fire,
and melted ice for her mother's use. This accom-
plished, she seated herself upon a low stool near the
bed and begged her mother to try and sleep a while.

"You are so tired," she whispered, "not once have
you closed your eyes since that dreadful hour last
night. See, I have straightened the willow bed in the
corner and spread everything soft upon it I could
find. Here is your jacket. Take off that pretty dress.
I'll fold it away very carefully and put it in the big
chest before you go to sleep."

Dame Brinker shook her head without turning her
eyes from her husband's face.

"I can watch, Mother," urged Gretel, "and I'll wake
you every time Father stirs. You are so pale, and your
eyes are so red — oh, Mother, *do!*"

The child pleaded in vain. Dame Brinker would
not leave her post.

Gretel looked at her in troubled silence, wondering
whether it was very wicked to care more for one
parent than for the other — and sure, yes, quite sure,

that she dreaded her father, while she clung to her mother with a love that was almost idolatry.

"Hans loves the father so well," she thought, "Why cannot I? Yet I could not help crying when I saw his hand bleed that day, last month, when he snatched the knife — and now, when he moans, how I ache, ache all over. Perhaps I love him after all, and God will see I am not such a bad, wicked girl as I thought. Yes, I love the poor father — almost as Hans does — not quite, for Hans is stronger and does not fear him.

"Oh, will that moaning go on forever and ever? Poor Mother, how patient she is; she almost never speaks about the money that went so strangely. If the father only could, just for one instant, open his eyes and tell us where the guilders went, I would not care for the rest. Yes, I would care; I don't want the poor father to die — I *know* I don't. Dear God, I don't want father to die."

Her thoughts merged into a prayer. When it ended, the poor child scarcely knew. Soon she found herself watching the fire. She watched it send a glow around the mother's form, tipping her faded skirt with light, and shedding a sort of newness over the thread-bare bodice. It was a relief to Gretel to see the lines in that weary face soften as the firelight flickered gently across it. Her thoughts ran on:

"Ah, if only Hans were here now, he could turn the father some way so the moans would stop. Oh dear! If this sickness lasts, we shall never skate any more. I must send my new skates back to the beautiful lady. Hans and I will not see the race," and Gretel's eyes, which had been dry before, grew full of tears.

"Never cry, child," said her mother soothingly. "This sickness may not be as bad as we think. The father has lain this way before."

Gretel sobbed now.

"Oh, Mother, it is not that alone — you do not know all — I am very, very bad and wicked!"

"*You*, Gretel? You, so patient and good!" and a bright, puzzled look beamed for an instant upon the child. "Hush, lovey, you'll wake him."

Gretel hid her face in her mother's lap and tried not to cry.

Her little hand, so thin and brown, lay in the coarse palm of her mother's, creased with many a hard day's work.

"The father tried to burn you — he did — I saw him, and he was *laughing!*"

"Hush, child!"

The mother's words came so suddenly and sharply that Raff Brinker, dead as he was to all that was passing around him, twitched slightly upon the bed.

Gretel said no more, but plucked drearily at the jagged edge of a hole in her mother's holiday gown. It had been burned there.

12. A Mighty Voice
and a Little Hero

Refreshed and rested, our boys came forth from the coffeehouse just as the big clock in the square was striking two.

Captain Peter was absorbed in thought, for Hans Brinker's sad story still echoed in his ears. Not until Ludwig rebuked him with a laughing, "Wake up, grandfather!" did he reassume his position as leader of the band.

"Ahem! This way, gentlemen!"

They were walking through the streets of the city. Haarlem, like Amsterdam, was gayer than usual, in honor of St. Nicholas.

"Do you see that red pincushion hanging on yonder door?" Lambert asked Ben.

"Yes."

"Well, that's a boy."

"A boy! What do you mean?"

"I mean that here in Haarlem, whenever a boy is

born, the parents have a red pincushion put out at the door. If it had been a girl instead of a boy, the cushion would have been white."

"Look!" almost screamed Ben, "there *is* a white cushion, at the door of that double-jointed house."

"True enough. I tell you what, captain," called out Lambert, slipping easily into Dutch, "we must get out of this street as soon as possible. It's full of babies! They'll set up a squall in a moment."

The captain laughed. "I'll take you to hear better music than that!" he said. "We are just in time to hear the organ at St. Bavon's. It's open today."

"What, the great Haarlem organ?" asked Ben, when Lambert had translated for him. "I have read of it, with its tremendous pipes, and its *vox humana*."

"The same," answered Lambert.

Someone was playing the organ as the boys entered the church, and a swell of sound rushed forth to meet them. Louder and louder it grew, like the roar of a mighty tempest, or the ocean pounding against the shore. In the midst of the tumult a tolling bell was heard; another answered, and another, and the storm paused as if to listen. The bells grew bolder; they rang out loud and clear.

Then, as the storm broke forth again with redoubled fury, came a scream — a terrible, musical scream! Was it man or demon? It was the *vox humana!*

At last an answer came — soft, tender, and loving.

The storm grew silent, and hidden birds filled the air with glad, ecstatic music. In the glorious hymn of thanksgiving that now arose, it seemed to Peter and Ben as if they were floating away on the music, with no wish but to hear forever those beautiful sounds.

Suddenly van Holp's sleeve was pulled impatiently, and a gruff voice beside him asked, "How long are you going to stay here, captain, blinking at the ceiling like a sick rabbit? It's high time we started."

"Hush!" whispered Peter, only half aroused.

"Come, man! Let's go," said Carl, giving the sleeve a second pull.

Peter turned reluctantly. All but Ben were casting reproachful glances on him.

"Well, boys," he whispered, "we will go. Softly now."

"That's the greatest thing I've seen or heard since I've been in Holland!" cried Ben enthusiastically, as soon as they reached the open air. "It's glorious!"

Peter understood English, though he did not speak it. He gave Ben a look that said plainly, he and Ben were not so very different after all, though one hailed from Holland and the other from England.

At the same hour that Ben was skating with his companions away from Haarlem toward Leyden, his younger sister and brother were at school in England, having their reading lesson.

"Master Robert Dobbs," said the teacher. He nodded at Ben's younger brother. "Begin on page 242." Robby read in a quick, childish voice:

The Hero of Haarlem

Many years ago, there lived in Haarlem, Holland, a boy whose father tended the sluice gates. These huge, oaken gates were placed at the entrances of the canals, and were raised or lowered to regulate the flow of water into the canals.

Because much of Holland is lower than the sea, the only way to keep the land from being flooded is by means of the sluice gates at the canals, and by the dykes—high banks or barriers. Both must be strong and solid to withstand the pressure of the flood tides.

Even children, like the boy in Haarlem long ago, know that constant watchfulness is needed to keep the waters from overwhelming the country, bringing ruin and death to all.

"Very good," said the teacher. "Now, Susan."

One lovely autumn afternoon, when the boy was about eight years old, he was sent by his parents to carry some cakes to a blind man who lived out in the country, near the dyke. After an hour with the old man, the boy bade him farewell and started on his homeward walk.

Trudging along by the canal, he noticed how the autumn rains had swollen the waters. Then he thought of his father's solid sluice gates and felt glad of their strength. "For," he said to himself, "if *they* should give way, these fields would be all covered with the angry waters. That's what father always calls them: *angry waters.*"

With these thoughts, the boy stooped to pick some flowers that grew along the way and to listen for the stealthy rustling of rabbits in the tall grass.

"Now Henry," said the teacher, nodding to the next reader.

Suddenly the boy looked around him in dismay. He had not noticed that the sun was setting; now it was growing dark, and he was still some distance from home.

Just as he was bracing himself for a run, he was startled by the sound of trickling water. Where did it come from? He looked up and saw a small hole in the dyke, through which a tiny stream was flowing. Any child in Holland will shudder at the thought of a *leak in the dyke!*

The boy understood the danger at a glance. That little hole, if the water were allowed to trickle through, would soon be a large one, and a terrible inundation would be the result.

Quick as a flash, the boy saw his duty. Throwing away his flowers, he clambered up the steep side of the dyke until he reached the hole, and thrust in his finger. The flowing was stopped! "There!" he thought. "The angry waters will stay back now! Haarlem shall not be drowned while *I* am here!"

This was all very well at first, but night was falling rapidly. Chill vapors filled the air. The boy began to tremble with cold and dread. He shouted loudly; he screamed, "Come here! Help!" But no one came. The cold grew more intense; a numbness commenced in his tired hand and crept up his arm, and soon his whole body was filled with pain. He shouted again, "Will no one come? Mother! Mother!" Alas, his mother, good practical soul, had already locked the doors, and had fully resolved to scold him on the morrow for spending the night with blind Jansen without her permission. He tried to whistle. Perhaps some straggling boy might heed the signal; but his teeth chattered so, it was impossible.

"Now Jenny Dobbs," said the teacher. Jenny's eyes were glistening, but she took a long breath and commenced:

The midnight moon looked down on the small, solitary form, crouched halfway up the dyke. His head was bent, but he was not asleep; for every now and then one restless hand rubbed feebly the outstretched arm that seemed fastened to the dyke, and often the pale, tearful face turned quickly at some real or fancied sound.

At daybreak a clergyman, returning from the bedside of a sick parishioner, thought he heard groans as he walked along the road on top of the dyke. Bending, he saw, far down on the side, a child apparently writhing in pain.

"In the name of wonder, boy," he exclaimed, "what are you doing there?"

"I am keeping the water from running in," answered the boy. "Tell them to come quick."

It is needless to add that they did come quickly and that —

"Jenny Dobbs," said the teacher, rather impatiently, "if you cannot control your feelings enough to read distinctly, we will wait until you can."

"Yes, sir!" said Jenny, quite startled.

It was strange, but at that very moment, far over the sea, Ben was saying to Lambert:

"The noble little fellow! I have often heard the story, but I never thought that it was true."

"True? Well, I have given you the story just as Mother told it to me, years ago; there is not a child in Holland who does not know it."

13. On the Canal

THE SKATING SEASON had commenced unusually early, and the boys were by no means alone on the ice. Whole families were skimming their way to Haarlem or Leyden or the neighboring villages. The ice was alive with people. Ben noticed the erect, easy carriage of the women and the picturesque variety of their costume.

There were belles from Leyden and fishwives from the border villages, cheese women from Gouda and prim matrons from beautiful countryseats on the Haarlemmer Meer, or Haarlem Lake. Gray-headed skaters were constantly to be seen, wrinkled old women with baskets upon their heads, and plump little toddlers on skates, clutching at their mothers' gowns. Some women carried their babies upon their backs, firmly secured with a bright shawl. The effect was pretty and graceful as they darted by or sailed slowly past, now nodding to an acquaintance, now throwing soft baby talk to the muffled little ones they carried.

Boys and girls were chasing each other and hiding behind the one-horse sleds that, loaded high with peat or timber, pursued their cautious way along the track marked out as "safe." A long file of young men, each grasping the coat of the one before him, flew by with electric speed.

Sometimes the ice squeaked under the chair of some gorgeous old dowager or rich burgomaster's lady. The chair would be laden with foot stoves and cushions. Mounted on shining runners, it slid along pushed by the sleepiest of servants.

As for the men, some were attired in ordinary citizen's dress; but many wore short woolen coats, wide breeches, and big silver buckles. Nearly all the men had pipes, and whizzed by puffing like locomotives.

Ben skated on in silence. There was so much to engage his attention that he almost forgot his companions. Part of the time he had been watching iceboats as they flew along over the ice. These boats had very large sails, set on a triangular frame furnished with iron runners, a rudder, and a brake. Some were small and easily managed by a boy. Others were large and beautiful; they carried gay pleasure parties and were manned by competent sailors. Ben was often startled at the swift approach of the resistless, high-winged things.

One huge iceboat, under full sail, came tearing down the canal. Ben saw its gilded prow, heard the skipper shout, and felt the great boom fairly whiz

over his head. The next instant he was spinning
some yards behind the great, skatelike rudder; the
boat has passed within an inch of his shoulder!

Lambert, who was near Ben, chided him roundly,
and for a while the two boys skated on in silence.
Peter and his companions finally caught up with them.

"That English lad is fleet enough," said Peter. "If
he were a born Hollander, he could do no better.
Halloo! Here you are too, van Mounen; why we hardly
hoped for the honor of meeting you again. What
were you fleeing from in such haste?"

"Snails!" retorted Lambert. "What kept you?"

"We have been talking; and besides, we halted
once to give Poot a chance to rest."

"He begins to look rather worn out," said Lambert
in a low voice.

Jacob, meanwhile, drew close to Ben. "I think we'd
better take a boat to Leyden," he said.

"Take a boat!" exclaimed Ben, in dismay. "Why,
man, our plan was to *skate* — not to be carried like
little children."

"Nonsense!" retorted Jacob. "It isn't being a baby
to go by boat!"

The boys laughed, but exchanged uneasy glances.
It would be great fun to jump on an iceboat, if they
had a chance; but to abandon so shamefully their
grand undertaking — who could think of such a thing?
An animated discussion arose at once.

Captain Peter brought his party to a halt. "It strikes

me," said he, "that we should consult Jacob's wishes
in this matter. He started the excursion, you know."

"Pooh!" sneered Carl, throwing a contemptuous
glance at Jacob. "Who's tired? We can rest all night
at Leyden."

Ludwig and Lambert looked anxious and disappointed. It was no slight thing to lose the credit of
having skated all the way from Broek to The Hague,
and back again, but both agreed that Jacob should decide the question.

"Good-natured, tired Jacob! He read the popular
sentiment at a glance. "Oh no," he said, in Dutch.
"I was joking. We will skate, of course."

The boys gave a delighted shout, and started on
again with renewed vigor. All but Jacob. He tried his
best not to seem fatigued, and, by not saying a word,
save his breath and energy for the great business of
skating. But in vain. Before long, the stout body grew
heavier and heavier — the white sails seemed to bow
and spin as they passed him, and he fell heavily on
the ice.

"Halloo!" cried van Mounen. "There goes Poot!"

Ben sprang hastily forward. "Jacob! Jacob, are you
hurt?"

Peter and Carl lifted the heavy boy. His face was
dead white. A crowd was collecting. Peter unbuttoned
Jacob's jacket, loosened his red scarf, and blew between the parted lips.

"Stand off, good people!" he cried. "Give him air!"

"Lay him down," called a woman from the crowd.

"Stand him upon his feet," shouted another.

"Give him wine," growled a stout fellow who was driving a loaded sled.

Ludwig and Lambert shouted in concert: "Wine, wine! Who has wine?"

A sleepy-eyed Dutchman began to fumble mysteriously under his heavy blue jacket.

"Wine, quick!" cried Peter, who, with Ben's help, was rubbing Jacob from head to foot.

Ludwig stretched forth his hand imploringly toward the fumbling Dutchman. "*Do* hurry! He will die!"

"He *is* dead!" cried an awful voice from among the bystanders. This startled the Dutchman.

"Have a care!" he said, reluctantly drawing forth a small blue flask. "This is schnapps. A little is enough."

A little *was* enough. The paleness gave way to a faint flush. Jacob opened his eyes and, half bewildered, half ashamed, feebly tried to free himself from those who were supporting him.

There was no alternative now but to have their exhausted friend carried to Leyden. By this time each boy had begun to entertain secret yearnings toward iceboats, and vowed not to desert Jacob. A gentle, steady breeze was setting southward. If only some accommodating skipper would come along now. . . .

Peter hailed the first sail that appeared; the men in

the stern would not even look at him. Three drays on
runners came along, but they were already loaded to
the utmost. Then an iceboat — a beautiful, tempting
little one — whizzed past like an arrow. The boys
had just time to look up eagerly when it was gone.
In despair, they resolved to prop up Jacob with their
strong arms, as well as they could, and take him to
the nearest village.

At that moment a very shabby iceboat came in
sight. With little hope of success, Peter hailed it.

The sail was lowered; then came the scraping sound
of the brake, and a pleasant voice called out from the
deck, "What now?"

"Will you take us on?" cried Peter, hurrying with
his companions as fast as he could, for the boat was
"bringing to" some distance ahead.

"How many?" the skipper asked.

"Six."

"Well, it's Saint Nicholas' Day — up with you! Young
gentleman sick?" He nodded toward Jacob.

"Yes — broke down — skated all the way from
Broek," answered Peter. "Do you go to Leyden?"

"That's as the wind says. It's blowing that way now.
Scramble up!"

Poor heavy Jacob! It was as much as the boys could
do to hoist him into the boat. All were in at last. The
skipper, puffing away at his pipe, let out the sail,
lifted the brake, and sat in the stern with folded
arms.

"Whew! How fast we go!" cried Ben. "This is something like! Feel better, Jacob?"

"Much better, thank you."

"Oh, you'll be as good as new in ten minutes. This makes a fellow feel like a bird."

Jacob nodded, and blinked his eyes.

"Don't go to sleep, Jacob," his cousin warned. "It's too cold. You might never wake up, you know. Persons often freeze to death in that way."

"I won't fall asleep," said Jacob confidently, and in two minutes he was snoring.

Carl and Ludwig laughed.

"We must wake him!" cried Ben. "It is dangerous, I tell you. Jacob! Ja-a-c —"

Captain Peter interfered, for three of the boys were helping Ben for the fun of the thing.

"Nonsense! Don't shake him! Let him alone. One never snores like that when one's freezing. Cover him up with something. Here, this cloak will do, hey, skipper?" and he looked toward the stern for permission to use it.

The man nodded.

"There," said Peter adjusting the garment, "let him sleep. He will be frisky as a lamb when he wakes. How far are we from Leyden, skipper?"

"Not more'n a couple of pipes," replied the skipper (puff! puff!). "Likely not more'n one an' a half" (puff! puff!) "if this wind holds" (puff! puff! puff!).

"What is the man saying, Lambert?" asked Ben,

who was holding his mittened hands against his cheeks to ward off the cutting wind.

"He says we're about two pipes from Leyden. Half the men here on the canal measure distances by the time it takes them to finish smoking a pipe."

It was grand — sailing, riding, or flying, whichever it was — and before they had time to draw a long breath, Leyden itself, with its high-peaked roofs, flew halfway to meet them.

When the city came in sight, it was high time to waken the sleeper. Jacob was quite restored and in excellent spirits. Peter, with hearty thanks, slipped some silver pieces into the skipper's tough, brown palm.

The sail soon came tumbling down. Scrape, scrape went the brake, scattering an ice shower round the boat.

"Good-bye, skipper!" shouted the boys, seizing their skates and leaping from the deck one by one. "Many thanks to you."

"Good-bye! Good-b— Here! Stop! I want my coat."

Ben was helping his cousin over the side of the boat. "What's the man shouting about? Oh, I know, you have his coat round your shoulders, Jacob."

"Now for an inn!" cried Peter, as they stepped into the city.

14. Mynheer Kleef and His Bill of Fare

IN LEYDEN, the boys soon found a small, unpretentious inn near the Breedestraat (Broad Street), with a painted lion over the door. This was the Red Lion, kept by Mynheer Kleef, a stout Dutchman with short legs and a very long pipe.

By this time the boys were ravenous. Lunch at Haarlem had only given them an appetite for more, and this had been heightened by their exercise and the swift sail on the canal.

"Come, mine host, give us what you can!" cried Peter.

"I can give you anything — everything," answered Mynheer Kleef, performing a difficult bow.

"Well, give us sausage and pudding."

"Ah, mynheer, the sausage is all gone. There is no pudding."

"Salmagundi, then, and plenty of it."

"That is out also, young master."

"Eggs?"

"Winter eggs are very poor eating," answered the innkeeper, puckering his lips and lifting his eyebrows.

"No eggs? Well — caviar."

The Dutchman raised his fat hands. "Caviar! That is made of gold! Who has caviar to sell?"

Peter had sometimes eaten it at home; he knew that it was made of the roe of sturgeon, or other large fish, but he had no idea of its cost.

"Well, mine host, what *have* you?"

"What have I? Everything. I have rye bread, sauerkraut, potato salad, and the fattest herring in Leyden."

"What do you say, boys?" asked the captain. "Will that do?"

"Yes," cried the famished youths, "if only he'll be quick."

Mynheer moved off like one walking in his sleep, but soon opened his eyes wide at the miraculous manner in which his herrings were made to disappear. Next came — or rather went — potato salad, rye bread, and coffee; then Utrecht water, flavored with orange, and finally slices of dry gingerbread. When his voracious young travelers started up, declaring they had eaten enough, he asked, "Will your worships have beds?"

"Will your worships have beds?" mocked Carl. "What do you mean? Do we look sleepy?"

"Not at all, master; but I would cause them to be

warmed and aired. None sleep under damp sheets at
the Red Lion."

"Ah, I understand. Shall we come back here to
sleep, captain?"

Peter was accustomed to finer lodgings, but this
was a frolic.

"Why not?" he replied. "We can fare excellently
here."

"Your worship speaks only the truth," said mynheer with great deference.

"How fine to be called 'your worship,'" laughed
Ludwig aside to Lambert, while Peter replied:

"Well, mine host, you may get the rooms ready by
nine."

"I have one beautiful chamber with three big beds
that will hold all of your worships," said mynheer
coaxingly.

"That will do."

"Whew!" whistled Carl when they reached the
street.

Ludwig started. "What now?"

"Nothing, only Mynheer Kleef of the Red Lion
little thinks how we shall make things spin in that
same room tonight. We'll set the bolsters flying!"

"Point of order!" cried Peter. "I must seek this
great Dr. Boekman before I sleep. If he is here in
Leyden, it will be no great task to find him, for he
always puts up at the Golden Eagle. While I'm looking

for him, what say you to walking with Ben up by the museum?"

"Agreed," said Ludwig and Lambert; but Jacob preferred to go with Peter. In vain Ben tried to persuade him to remain at the inn and rest. He declared that he had never felt better and wished to take a look at the city, for it was his first visit to Leyden.

"Here we are at the corner. Remember, we all meet back at the Red Lion for supper at eight," said the captain, as he and Jacob walked away.

15. The Red Lion Becomes Dangerous

THE BOYS WERE GLAD to find a blazing fire awaiting them upon their return to the Red Lion. Peter and Jacob had inquired in vain concerning Dr. Boekman. All they could find out was that he had been seen in Haarlem that morning.

"As for his being in Leyden," the landlord of the Golden Eagle had said to Peter, "the thing is impossible. He always lodges here when in town. By this time there would be a crowd at my door waiting to consult him."

He added sharply, "Come now, what more do you wish? Supper? Beds?"

"No, mynheer, I am just seeking Dr. Boekman."

"Go look for him elsewhere. He is not in Leyden."

Peter was not to be put off. After a few more rough words, he obtained permission to leave a note for the famous surgeon, and a promise that it should be promptly delivered when Dr. Boekman arrived. Peter and Jacob had then returned to the Red Lion.

This inn had once been a fine house, the home of a rich burgher; but having grown old and shabby, it had passed through many hands, and finally into the possession of Mynheer Kleef.

The public room on the ground floor was the landlord's joy and pride. There everything was Dutch neatness and order.

It was a large, bare room; its tile floor of red and yellow squares looked like a vast checkerboard. A dozen high-backed wooden chairs stood around; the great blazing fireplace had a tiled hearth; and high above it was a narrow mantelshelf, filled with shining brass candlesticks, pipe lighters, and tinderboxes.

At one end of the room there were three pine tables; at the other, a dresser filled with mugs, dishes, pipes, tankards, and bottles — all guarded by a brass-hooped keg standing on legs.

Two sleepy, shabby-looking men in wooden shoes were seated near the glowing fireplace, hugging their knees and smoking short, stumpy pipes. In the corner lay a heap of skates, and six tired, well-dressed boys in various attitudes sprawled on the wooden chairs. This was the coffee room of the Red Lion as it appeared at nine o'clock on the evening of December 6, 18—.

The boys had been ravenous enough to eat all the food they could get for supper — Dutch sausage, rye bread, pickles, and coffee. They laughed and talked a while after the meal, and counted their money by way of settling a discussion over their expenses. Then the captain marched his company off to bed.

One of the ill-favored men by the fire had shuffled toward the dresser and was ordering a mug of beer just as Ludwig, who brought up the rear, was stepping from the public room.

"I don't like that fellow's eye," he whispered to Carl. "He looks just like one of those men in the the painting, 'The Voetspoelen.'"

"Pooh!" sneered Carl, "I knew it. That picture was too much for you. Look sharp now, and see if yon fellow with the candle doesn't look like the other villain."

"No, indeed, his face is as honest as a Gouda cheese. But, I say, Carl, that really was a horrid picture."

"Humph! What did you stare at it so long for?"

"I couldn't help it."

By this time the boys had reached the "beautiful room with three beds in it." A dumpy little maiden with long earrings met them at the doorway and dropped them a curtsy as she left. She was carrying a long-handled thing that resembled a frying pan with a cover.

"I am glad to see that," said van Mounen to Ben. "What?"

"Why, the warming pan. It's full of hot ashes; she's been heating our beds."

"Oh! a warming pan, eh! Much obliged to her, I'm

sure," said Ben, too sleepy to make any further comment.

Meantime Ludwig still talked of the picture. He had seen it in a shop window during their evening walk. It showed two men tied back to back, standing on shipboard, surrounded by a group of seamen who were preparing to cast them together into the sea. (This mode of putting prisoners to death was called *voetspoelen,* or "feet washing," and was practiced by the Dutch upon the pirates of Dunkirk in 1605.) Bad as the painting was, the expression upon the pirates' faces had been well done. Sullen and despairing as they seemed, they wore such a cruel, malignant aspect that Ludwig had felt a secret satisfaction in their fate. He might have forgotten the scene by this time but for that ill-looking man by the fire. Now, he inwardly hoped that voetspoelen would not haunt his dreams.

"Good night!" said Peter's voice from under the covers.

"Good night," called back everybody but Jacob, who already lay snoring beside the captain.

It was the middle of the night. Little squares of moonlight were slowly moving across the bare, polished floor of the boys' room. Something else was moving also — not quite so slowly, but quite as stealthily.

During the early hours of the night, Jacob Poot had been gradually but surely winding himself in all the bed covers. He now lay like a monster chrysalis beside the half-frozen Peter, who, accordingly, was skating with all his might over the coldest, bleakest of dreamland icebergs. In his dream, Peter slid a few thousand feet from one iceberg to another, and the shock woke him.

Whew! How cold he was! He gave a hopeless, desperate tug at the chrysalis. In vain: sheet, blanket, and spread were firmly wound about Jacob's inanimate form. Peter looked drowsily toward the window.

"Clear moonlight," he thought. "We shall have pleasant weather tomorrow. Halloo! what's that?"

He saw the moving thing, or rather something black crouching upon the floor, for it had halted as Peter stirred. He watched in silence. Soon it moved again, nearer and nearer. It was a man crawling on his hands and feet!

The captain's first impulse was to call out, but he took an instant to consider matters. The creeper had a shining knife in one hand!

Peter was naturally self-possessed. When the head turned toward the bed, Peter's eyes closed as if in sleep; but when it turned away, nothing could be keener, sharper, than the captain's gaze.

Closer, closer crept the man. His back was very close to Peter now. The knife was laid softly upon the floor; one careful arm reached forth stealthily to drag the clothes from the chair by the captain's bed — he was going to rob them!

Now it was Peter's turn. Holding his breath, he sprang up and leaped with all his strength on the robber's back, stunning him with the force of the blow. To seize the knife was but a second's work. The robber began to struggle, but Peter sat like a giant astride the prostrate form.

"If you stir," said the boy in as terrible a voice as he could command, "stir but one inch, I will plunge this knife into your neck. Ben! van Mounen! wake up!" he shouted, still pressing down the robber's head, and holding the knife at pricking distance. "Give me a hand! I've got him!"

The chrysalis rolled over, but made no other sign.

"Up, everyone!" cried Peter, never budging. "Ludwig! Lambert! Thunder! Are you all dead?"

Dead? Not they! Van Mounen and Ben were on their feet in an instant. "Hey? What now?" they shouted.

"I've got a robber here," said Peter coolly. "Lie still, you scoundrel, or I'll slice your head off! — Cut out the bed cord, Ludwig. Plenty of time; he's a dead man if he stirs."

The man growled and swore, but dared not move.

Ludwig was already up and reaching in his breeches pocket for his jackknife, the pride of his heart. It could do good service now. The boys bared the bedstead in a moment. It was laced backward and forward with a rope.

"I'll cut it," cried Ludwig, sawing away at the knot, "Hold him tight, Peter!"

"Never fear!" answered the captain, giving the robber a warning prick.

The boys were soon pulling at the rope like good fellows. It was out at last — a long, stout piece.

"Now, boys," commanded the captain, "lift up his arms! Cross his hands over his back! That's right — tie them tight!"

"Yes, and his feet too, the villain!" cried the boys in great excitement, tying the knots with hard jerks.

The prisoner changed his tone. "Oh — oh!" he moaned, "Spare a poor, sick man. I was but walking in my sleep."

"Ugh!" grunted Lambert, still tugging away at the rope. "Asleep, were you? Well, we'll wake you up."

"The man uttered fierce oaths between his teeth, then cried in a piteous voice, "Unbind me, good young masters! I have five little children at home. By Saint Bavon I swear to give you each a ten-guilder piece if you will but free me!"

"Ha, ha!" laughed the boys.

Then came threats — threats that made Ludwig fairly shudder, though he continued to bind and tie with redoubled energy.

"Hold up, mynheer housebreaker!" said van Mounen in a warning voice. "That knife is very near

your throat. If you make the captain nervous, there is
no telling what may happen."

The robber took the hint, and fell into a sullen
silence.

Just at this moment the chrysalis upon the bed
stirred and sat erect.

"What's the matter?" asked Jacob, without opening
his eyes.

"Matter!" echoed Ludwig, half trembling, half
laughing. "Get up, Jacob. Here's work for you. Come
sit on this fellow's back while we get into our clothes;
we're half perished with cold!"

"What fellow? Donder!"

"Hurrah for Poot!" cried all the boys, as Jacob
slid quickly to the floor, bedclothes and all, and sat
heavily on the robber's back.

"No use in holding him down any longer, boys,"
said Peter rising, but bending as he did so to draw
a pistol from the man's belt. "You see, I've been keeping guard over this pretty little weapon for the last
ten minutes. It's cocked, and the least wriggle might
have set it off. No danger now. I must dress. You and I,
Lambert, will go for the police."

"Where is Carl?" asked one of the boys.

They looked at one another. Carl certainly was not
among them.

"Oh!" cried Ludwig, frightened at last, "where is
he? Perhaps he's had a fight with the robber and got
killed."

"Not a bit of it," said Peter quietly, as he buttoned his stout jacket. "Look under the beds."

They did so. Carl was not there.

Just then they heard a commotion on the stairway. Ben hastened to open the door. The landlord almost tumbled in; he was armed with a big blunderbuss. Two or three lodgers followed; then the daughter, with an upraised frying pan in one hand and a candle in the other; and behind her, looking pale and frightened, was Carl!

"There's your man, mine host," said Peter nodding toward the prisoner.

Mine host raised his blunderbuss, the girl screamed, and Jacob, more nimble than usual, rolled quickly from the robber's back.

"Don't fire," cried Peter, "he is tied, hand and foot. Let's roll him over and see what he looks like."

Carl stepped briskly forward, with a blustering "Yes. We'll turn him over in a way he won't like. Lucky we've caught him!"

"Ha, ha!" laughed Ludwig. "Where were you, Master Carl?"

"Where was I?" retorted Carl angrily. "Why, I went to give the alarm, to be sure!"

All the boys exchanged glances, but they were too happy and elated to say anything ill-natured. Carl certainly was bold enough now. He took the lead, and three others helped to turn over the helpless man.

While the robber lay, face up, scowling and muttering, Ludwig took the candlestick from the girl's hand.

"I must have a good look at the beauty," he said, drawing closer, but the words were no sooner spoken than he turned pale and started so violently that he almost dropped the candle.

" 'The voetspoelen'!" he cried. "Why, boys, it's the man who sat by the fire!"

"Of course it is," answered Peter. "We counted our money before him like simpletons."

The landlord's daughter had left the room. She now ran in, holding a pair of huge wooden shoes. "See, Father," she cried, "here are his great boats. It's the man that we put in the next room after the young masters went to bed. Ah, it was wrong to send the poor young gentlemen up here so far out of sight and sound."

"The scoundrel!" hissed the landlord. "He has disgraced my house. I'll go for the police at once!"

In less than fifteen minutes two drowsy-looking officers were in the room. After telling Mynheer Kleef that he must appear early in the morning with the boys and make his complaint before a magistrate, they marched off with their prisoner.

It was ten o'clock when Captain Peter and his band came straggling down for breakfast, one by one. The landlord's daughter had bestirred herself to prepare them a good meal.

"A pretty hour," said the landlord gruffly. "It is high time we were before the court. Fine business this for a respectable inn. You will testify truly, young masters, that you found most excellent fare and lodgment at the Red Lion?"

"Of course we will," answered Carl saucily, "and pleasant company, too, though they visit at rather unseasonable hours."

A stare was all the answer mynheer made to this, but the daughter, shaking her earrings at Carl, said sharply, "Not so very pleasant either, master traveler, if one could judge by the way *you* ran away from it!"

"Impertinent creature!" hissed Carl under his breath.

After breakfast, the boys went to the Police Court, accompanied by Mynheer Kleef and his daughter. Mynheer's testimony was to the effect that a robber at the Red Lion had been unheard of until last night. The Red Lion was a most respectable inn — as respectable as any house in Leyden.

Each boy in turn told all he knew of the affair, and identified the prisoner in the box as the same man who entered their room in the dead of night. Peter and the rest testified that the man had not moved a muscle from the moment the point of the dagger touched his throat until, bound from head to foot, he was rolled over for inspection.

The landlord's daughter declared that, "if it hadn't been for that handsome young gentleman there," pointing to Peter, they "might have all been murdered in their beds: for the dreadful man had a great shining knife most as long as your honor's arm."

Finally, after a little questioning and cross-questioning from the public prosecutor, the witnesses were dismissed and the robber was handed over to the consideration of the Criminal Court.

"The scoundrel!" said Carl savagely, when the boys reached the street. "If I had been in your place, Peter, I certainly should have killed him outright!"

"He was fortunate, then, in falling into gentler hands," was Peter's quiet reply. "It appears he has been arrested before under a charge of housebreaking. He did not succeed in robbing this time, but he broke the door fastenings, and that I believe makes it a burglary in the eye of the law. He was armed with a knife, too, and that makes it worse for him, poor fellow."

"All right," Peter said then, briskly. "Where would you all like to go?"

"To the Egyptian Museum," answered Lambert, after holding a brief consultation with Ben.

"That is on the Breedestraat. To the museum, then."

16. Leyden

THE BOYS WERE SOON EXAMINING the museum's rich collection of ancient Egyptian life. There were household utensils, clothing, weapons, and musical instruments. There were sarcophagi, or decorated coffins, and mummies of men, women, and cats. Here was a massive gold armlet that an Egyptian king had worn, and there the jewels and trinkets of a Pharoah's daughter.

When the boys left the Egyptian Museum, they stood again on the Breedestraat, the longest and finest street in Leyden. It had no canal running through it, and elegant houses, painted in every variety of color, stood with their gable ends to the street.

The city of Leyden is intersected by numerous waterways formed by the river Rhine, and more than a hundred and fifty stone bridges link the streets across the canals. The Rhine also forms a moat around Leyden; it is crossed by drawbridges at the imposing gateways that give access to the city. Fine, broad promenades, shaded by noble trees, border the canals and give an air of scholarly seclusion to the place.

Ben, as he scanned the buildings on the Rapenburg Canal, was somewhat disappointed in the appearance of the great University of Leyden. But when he remembered the famous men in religion, learning, and science who had once studied there, he was quite willing to forego architectural beauty.

Peter and Jacob regarded the building with more practical interest, for they were to enter it as students in a few months.

After lunch, and then dinner, the boys sat warming themselves at the inn, waiting for Peter. He had gone on another fruitless search for Dr. Boekman. When he returned, the boys once more prepared for skating. They were thirteen miles from The Hague, and the ice was excellent.

17. The Merchant Prince
and Princess

As THE BOYS SKATED ONWARD, they saw a number
of great, formal houses, with elaborate gardens,
square hedges, and wide ditches — some crossed by
a bridge. These ditches were everywhere, and shone
in the sunlight like trailing ribbons of glass.

Twelve miles were passed. A few more long strokes
would take them to The Hague.

Never had a sunset appeared more beautiful to
Peter than when he saw it reflected in the windows
and shining roofs of the city before him. Never had
The Hague itself seemed more inviting. He was no
longer Peter van Holp going to visit a great city.
He was a knight, an adventurer, approaching the
enchanted castle where luxury and ease awaited him,
for his own sister's house was not half a mile away.

Well might Peter feel that his sister's house was
like an enchanted castle. Large and elegant it was;

the very lion crouching at its gate seemed a creature
turned to stone through magic. And within were
genii — servants who sprang silently forth at the sum-
mons of bell or knocker.

The boys received the heartiest of welcomes. After
they had talked a while with their lively hostess,
Peter's sister, they were summoned to a grand repast.

Now, they had their caviar and salmagundi, as well
as sausage and cheese, besides salad, fruit, and cake.

Of course Peter's sister soon heard all about the
boys' adventures. How they had skated over forty
miles and seen rare sights on the way; how they had
lost their purse and found it again; how one of the
party had fallen and given them an excuse for a sail
in an iceboat; how, above all, they had caught a
robber, and so for a second time saved their slippery
purse.

"And now, Peter," said the lady, when the story
was finished, "you must write at once to tell the good
people of Broek that your adventures have reached
their height, for you and your fellow travelers have
all been taken prisoners."

The boys looked startled.

"Indeed, I shall do no such thing," laughed Peter.
"We must leave tomorrow at noon."

But his sister had already decided differently; it
was finally settled that they should remain at The
Hague for at least two days.

Next they talked of the great skating race. Peter's

sister promised to be present. "I shall witness your triumph, Peter," she said, "for you are the fastest skater I ever knew."

Peter blushed and gave a slight cough, as Carl answered for him.

"Ah, mevrouw, he is swift, but all the Broek boys are fine skaters — even the ragpickers." And he thought bitterly of poor Hans.

The lady laughed. "That will make the race all the more exciting," she said. "But I shall wish each of you to be the winner."

At this moment her husband, Mynheer van Gend, came in. His frank, "Well, now, this is pleasant," as he shook hands with them all, made the boys feel quite at home.

Ben noticed with pleasure the English books lying upon the table. He saw also, over the carved, upright piano, life-sized portraits of the Dutch-born William of Orange and his English queen — a sight that, for a time, brought England and Holland side by side in his heart.

Next, mynheer showed the boys some exquisite iron jewelry — beautiful medallions designed from rare paintings, and bordered with fine tracery and openwork. Worthy, he said, of being worn by the fairest lady of the land. Consequently the necklace was handed with a bow and smile to Mevrouw van Gend.

It was hard to break up so pleasant a party, but the van Gend household moved with the regularity of clockwork. There was no lingering when the cordial "good night!" was spoken.

Rooms with three beds in them were not to be found in *this* mansion. Some of the rooms contained two, but each visitor had his own bed.

Tired as he was, Ben thought how his mother and sister Jenny would exclaim over the fine bed coverings — the pillow spread trimmed with costly lace, and embroidered with a gorgeous crest and initial; the dekbed cover — a great silk bag, large as the bed, stuffed with swan's-down; and the pink satin quilts, embroidered with garlands of flowers.

He decided to send home a description, in his next letter, of his room. Its floor was nearly covered with a rich carpet bordered with thick black fringe. Hung with tapestry, its walls were of crimson silk, topped with a gilded cornice which shot down gleams of light.

Peter was up first the next morning; knowing the punctual habits of his brother-in-law, he took good care that none of the boys should oversleep.

While Jacob was dressing, Peter wrote to Broek of their safe arrival at The Hague. He begged his mother to send word to Hans Brinker: Dr. Boekman had not yet reached Leyden, but a letter containing Hans's message had been left at the hotel in Leyden where the doctor always stayed. "Tell Hans," wrote Peter, "that I shall call there again, as I pass through Leyden."

"You know, Mother," added Peter, "that I have always considered sister van Gend's house as rather quiet and lonely; but I assure you, it is not so now. Sister says our presence has warmed it for the whole winter. Brother van Gend has promised to let Ben and me ride on his noble black horses. They are gentle as kittens, he says, if one has a firm touch at the rein. He will lend Jacob his English pony and obtain three extra horses for the others, and all of us are to trot about the city, in a grand cavalcade led by him. Ludwig has given us a name already: the Broek Cavalry."

The Broek Cavalry was not disappointed. Mynheer van Gend readily procured good horses, and all the boys could ride. They saw The Hague to their hearts' content.

On their return, they gathered in the family sitting room, around the great porcelain stove. It was so very large, it seemed to send out warmth by the houseful, and its pure white sides and polished brass rings were pleasant to look upon.

To describe all the boys saw and did on that day and the next would be impossible. But they quite delighted Mynheer van Gend, for a merrier, more observant party never went sight-seeing.

The boys' visit to The Hague came to an end at last. They had spent three happy days and nights with the van Gends, and had not once, in all that time, put on skates.

18. Homeward Bound

ON MONDAY MORNING, bright and early, the boys bade farewell to their hosts and started on their homeward journey.

Peter lingered a while at the lion-guarded door, for he and his sister had many parting words to say.

Ludwig had taken his share of the farewell in the most matter-of-fact manner possible, and though he loved his sister, he had winced a little at her making such a child of him as to put an extra kiss "for Mother" upon his forehead.

He was already on the canal with Carl and Jacob. They were so happy to be on skates once more, so impatient to dart at once into the very heart of Broek, that they spun and wheeled about like crazy fellows until the captain, and Ben and Lambert, joined them at last. Soon they were skimming along the canal.

Very little was said for the first half-hour. Each did his best, flying, with bent body and eager eyes, in and out among the placid skaters on the canal, until the very guard shouted to them to "Hold up!" This only served to send them onward with a power that startled all beholders.

After a while Jacob slackened his speed — then Ludwig — then Lambert — then Carl.

They soon halted to take a long breath, and finally found themselves standing in a group gazing after Peter and Ben, who were still racing in the distance as if their lives were at stake.

"It is very evident," said Lambert, as he and his three companions started on again, "that neither of them will give up until he can't help it."

"What foolishness!" growled Carl, "to tire themselves at the beginning of the journey. They're racing in earnest, that's certain. Halloo! Peter's flagging!"

"Not so!" cried Ludwig. "Catch him being beaten!"

"Ha, ha!" sneered Carl. "I tell you, boy, Benjamin is ahead."

Ludwig grew indignant at once. "*Now* look and see if Peter isn't ahead!"

"I think he is," interposed Lambert, but I can't quite tell at this distance."

"He can't be — for Ben is ahead!" insisted Carl. "Gunst! That iceboat will run over him. No — he is clear! They're a couple of geese anyhow. Hurray! they're at the turn. Who's ahead?"

"Peter!" cried Ludwig joyfully.

"Good for the captain!" shouted Lambert and Jacob.

This turn in the canal had evidently been their goal, for the two racers came to a sudden halt after passing it.

Ben was looking at Peter with mingled vexation, admiration, and surprise as the boys drew near.

They heard him saying in English:

"You're a perfect bird on the ice, Peter van Holp. The first fellow that ever beat me in a fair race, I can tell you!"

Peter, who understood the language better than he could speak it, returned a laughing bow at Ben's compliment, but made no further reply.

"You are beaten, though, my boy," said Lambert in English, "and fairly, too. How will it be, I wonder, on the day of the grand race?"

Ben flushed, and gave a proud, defiant laugh, as if to say:

"This was mere pastime. I'm determined to beat then, come what will!"

19. Boys and Girls

By THE TIME the boys reached the village of Voor-hout, which stands near the grand canal, about half-way between The Hague and Haarlem, they were forced to hold a council. The wind, though moderate at first, had grown steadily stronger, and now they could hardly skate against it.

"No use trying to face such a blow as this," said Ludwig. "It cuts its way down a man's throat like a knife."

Just then a gust came that nearly threw the strong-chested Carl; it almost strangled Jacob and quite up-set Ludwig.

"That settles it!" shouted Peter. "Off with your skates! We'll go into Voorhout."

At Voorhout they found a little inn with a big yard that was provided with a complete set of skittles.

First a hearty dinner, then the bowling game. With pins as long as their arms, balls as big as their heads, plenty of strength for rolling, and a clean sweep of sixty yards, no wonder the boys were happy.

That night Captain Peter and his men slept soundly; no prowling robber came to disturb them. In the morning they ate such a breakfast that the landlord asked them where they "belonged." When they said "Broek," he made up his mind that the Broek people starved their children.

Fortunately, the wind had tired itself out and fallen asleep in the great sea cradle beyond the dunes. There were signs of snow; otherwise, the weather was fine.

It was mere child's play for the boys, now well rested, to skate to Leyden. Here they halted a while for Peter's errand at the Golden Eagle. He left the city with a lightened heart; Dr. Boekman had been at the hotel, read the note containing Hans's message, and departed for Broek.

There were not many upon the canal that day between Leyden and Haarlem. However, as the boys neared Amsterdam, they found themselves once more in the midst of a moving throng. The big icebreaker had been at work for the first time that season, but there was still plenty of skating ground left yet.

"Three cheers for home!" cried van Mounen, as they crossed the Y onto the Broek canal.

They reached Lambert's home first.

"Good-bye, boys!" he cried, as he left them. "We've had the greatest time in all Holland."

"So we have. Good-bye, van Mounen!" answered the

others. Peter hailed him. "I say, van Mounen, classes begin tomorrow."

"I know it. Our holiday is over. Good-bye again."

"Good-bye!"

Broek came in sight. Such meetings! Katrinka was on the canal — Carl was delighted. Hilda was there — Peter felt rested in an instant. Rychie was there — Ludwig and Jacob nearly knocked each other over in their eagerness to shake hands with her.

Annie Bouman was also on the canal, looking even prettier than the other maidens, in her graceful peasant's costume. But she did not mingle with Rychie's party; neither did she look unusually happy.

The one she wanted most to see was not among the newcomers. Indeed, he was not on the canal at all. She had not been near Broek since the eve of Saint Nicholas, for she was staying with her sick grandmother in Amsterdam and had been granted a brief resting spell, as the grandmother called it, because she had been such a faithful little nurse night and day.

Annie had devoted her resting spell to skating with all her might toward Broek and back again, in the hope of meeting some of her family, or Gretel Brinker, on the canal. Not one of them had she seen, and she must hurry back without even a glimpse of her mother's cottage; for the poor helpless grandmother, she knew, was by this time moaning for someone to turn her upon her cot.

"Where can Gretel be?" thought Annie, as she flew over the ice. "She can almost always steal a few moments from her work at this time of day. Poor Gretel! What a dreadful thing it must be to have a dull father! I should be woefully afraid of him, I know — so strong, and yet so strange!"

Annie had not heard of his illness. Dame Brinker and her affairs received but little notice from the people of the place.

If Gretel had not been known as a goose-girl, she might have had more friends among the peasantry of the neighborhood. As it was, Annie Bouman was the only one who did not feel ashamed to avow herself by word and deed the companion of Gretel and Hans.

When the neighbors' children laughed at her for keeping such poor company, she would simply flush when Hans was ridiculed, or laugh in a careless, disdainful way; but to hear little Gretel abused always awakened her wrath.

"Goose-girl, indeed!" she would say. "I can tell you any of you are fitter for the work than she. My father often said last summer that it troubled him to see such a bright-eyed, patient little maiden tending geese. Humph! She would not harm them, as you would, Janzoon Kolp; and she would not tread upon them, as you might, Kate Wouters."

This would be pretty sure to start a laugh at the clumsy, ill-natured Kate's expense, and Annie would walk loftily away from the group of young gossips.

Perhaps some memory of Gretel's assailants crossed her mind as she skated rapidly toward Amsterdam, for her eyes flashed ominously and she more than once gave her pretty head a defiant toss.

There were five joyous households in Broek that night.

The boys were back safe and sound; and they found all well at home.

But the next morning! Ah, how stupidly school bells will ding-dong, ding-dong, when one is tired.

20. The Crisis

In the Brinker cottage there is the same sad group, just as it was four days ago. No, not precisely the same, for Raff Brinker is paler; his fever is gone, though he knows nothing of what is passing. *Then* they were alone in the bare, clean room. *Now* there is another group in an opposite corner.

Dr. Boekman is there, talking in a low tone with a stout young man who listens intently. The stout young man is his student and assistant. Hans is there also. He stands near the window, respectfully waiting until he shall be accosted.

"You see, Vollenhoven," said Dr. Boekman, "it is a clear case of —" and here he went off into a queer jumble of Latin and Dutch.

After a while, as Vollenhoven looked at him rather blankly, the learned man condescended to speak to him in simpler words.

"It is probably like Rip Donderdunck's case," he explained, in a low, mumbling tone. "He fell from the top of Voppelploot's windmill. After the accident the

man was stupid, and finally became idiotic. In time
he lay helpless like yon fellow on the bed; moaned
too, like him, and kept constantly lifting his hand to
his head. My learned friend von Choppem performed
an operation upon this Donderdunck, and discovered
under the skull a small dark sac which pressed upon
the brain. This had been the cause of the trouble.
My friend von Choppem removed it — a splendid
operation! You see, according to Celsus —" and here
the doctor again went off into Latin.

"Did the man live?" asked the assistant respectfully.

Dr. Boekman scowled. "That is of no consequence.
I believe he died, but why not fix your mind on the
grand features of the case? Consider a moment how
— " and he plunged into Latin mysteries more deeply
than ever.

"But, mynheer," gently persisted the student, who
knew that the doctor would not rise to the surface
for hours unless pulled at once from his favorite
depths. "Mynheer, you have other engagements today: three legs in Amsterdam, you remember, and an
eye in Broek, and that tumor up the canal."

"The tumor can wait," said the doctor reflectively.
The doctor by this time was speaking aloud. He had
quite forgotten where he was.

Vollenhoven made another attempt.

"This poor fellow on the bed, mynheer. Do you
think you can save him?"

"Ah, indeed, certainly," stammered the doctor, suddenly perceiving that he had been talking rather off the point. "Certainly — that is, I hope so."

"If anyone in Holland can, mynheer," murmured the assistant with honest bluntness, "it is yourself."

The doctor looked displeased, growled out a request for the student to talk less, and beckoned Hans to draw near.

This strange man had a great horror of speaking to women, especially on surgical matters. "One can never tell," he said, "what moment the creatures will scream or faint." Therefore he explained Raff Brinker's case to Hans and told him what he believed should be done to save the patient.

Hans listened attentively, growing red and pale by turns, and throwing anxious glances toward the bed.

"It may *kill* the father — did you say, mynheer?" he exclaimed at last, in a trembling whisper.

"It may, my boy. But I have a strong belief that it will cure and not kill. A great operation is proposed," Dr. Boekman went on indignantly, "but one might as well do it with a hatchet. The only question asked is, 'Will it kill?'"

"The question is everything to us, mynheer," said Hans, with tearful dignity.

Dr. Boekman looked at him in sudden dismay.

"Ah! Exactly so. You are right, boy, I am a fool. Good boy. One does not wish one's father killed — of course not. I am a fool."

"Will he die, mynheer, if this sickness goes on?"

"Humph! This is no new illness. The same thing growing worse every instant — pressure on the brain — will take him off soon, like *that*," said the doctor, snapping his fingers.

"And the operation *may* save him," pursued Hans. "How soon, mynheer, can we know?"

Dr. Boekman grew impatient.

"In a day, perhaps an hour. Talk with your mother, boy, and let her decide. My time is short."

Hans approached his mother; at first, when she looked up at him, he could not utter a syllable; then turning his eyes away he said in a firm voice:

"I must speak with the mother alone."

Quick little Gretel, who could not quite understand what was passing, threw an indignant look at Hans and walked away.

"Come back, Gretel, and sit down," said Hans sorrowfully. She obeyed.

Dame Brinker and her boy stood by the window while the doctor and his assistant, bending over the bedside, conversed together in a low tone. There was no danger of disturbing the patient. He appeared like one blind and deaf. Only his faint, piteous moans showed him to be a living man. Hans was talking earnestly, and in a low voice, for he did not wish his sister to hear.

With dry, parted lips, Dame Brinker leaned toward him searching his face, as if suspecting a meaning beyond his words. Once she gave a quick, frightened sob that made Gretel start, but after that she listened calmly.

When Hans ceased to speak, his mother turned, gave one agonized look at her husband lying there so pale and unconscious, and threw herself on her knees beside the bed.

Poor little Gretel! What did all this mean? She looked with questioning eyes at Hans — he was standing, but his head was bent as if in prayer; at the doctor — he was gently feeling her father's head and looked like one examining some curious stone; at the assistant — the man coughed and turned away; at her mother. Gretel knelt beside her mother, twined her arms about her neck, and prayed desperately.

When the mother arose, Dr. Boekman, with a show of trouble in his eyes, asked gruffly, "Well, juffrouw, shall it be done?"

"Will it pain him, mynheer?" she asked in a trembling voice.

"I cannot say. Probably not. Shall it be done?"

"It may *cure* him, you said, and — mynheer, did you tell my boy that — perhaps — perhaps —" she could not finish.

"Yes, juffrouw, I said the patient might sink under the operation, but we will hope it may prove otherwise." He looked at his watch. The assistant moved impatiently to the window. "Come, juffrouw, time presses. Yes or no?"

Hans wound his arm about his mother. It was not his usual way. He even leaned his head against her shoulder.

"The meester awaits an answer," he whispered.

Dame Brinker had long been the head of her house in every sense. Many a time she had been very stern with Hans, ruling him with a strong hand, and rejoicing in her motherly discipline; now she felt so weak, so helpless. It was something to feel that firm embrace. There was strength even in the touch of that yellow hair.

She turned to her boy imploringly.

"Oh, Hans! What shall I say?"

"Say what God tells thee, Mother," answered Hans, bowing his head.

One quick questioning prayer to Heaven rose from the mother's heart. The answer came.

She turned toward Dr. Boekman.

"It is right, mynheer. I consent."

"Humph!" grunted the doctor, as if to say, "You've been long enough about it." Then he conferred a moment with his assistant, who listened with great outward deference, but was inwardly rejoicing at the grand joke he would have to tell his fellow students. He had actually seen a tear in "old Boekman's" eye.

Meanwhile Gretel looked on in trembling silence; but when she saw the doctor open a leathern case, and take out one sharp, gleaming instrument after another, she sprang forward.

"Oh, Mother! The poor father meant no wrong. Are they going to murder him?"

"I do not know, child," screamed Dame Brinker, looking fiercely at Gretel. "I do not know."

"This will not do, juffrouw," said Dr. Boekman sternly, and at the same time he cast a quick, penetrating look at Hans. "You and the girl must leave the room. The boy may stay."

Dame Brinker drew herself up in an instant. Her eyes flashed. Her whole countenance was changed. She looked like one who had never wept, never felt a moment's weakness. Her voice was low but decided. "I stay with my husband, mynheer."

Dr. Boekman looked astonished. His orders were seldom disregarded in this style. For an instant his eye met hers.

"You may remain, juffrouw," he said in an altered voice.

Gretel had already disappeared.

In one corner of the cottage was a small closet where her rough, boxlike bed was fastened against the wall: none would think of the trembling little creature crouching there in the dark.

Dr. Boekman took off his heavy coat; he filled an earthen basin with water and placed it near the bed. Then turning to Hans he asked, "Can I depend upon you, boy?"

"You can, mynheer."

"I believe you. Stand at the head, here. Your

mother may sit at your right — so," and he set a chair near the cot.

"Remember, juffrouw, there must be no cries, no fainting."

Dame Brinker answered him with a look.

He was satisfied. "Now, Vollenhoven."

Oh, that case with the terrible instruments! The assistant lifted them. Gretel, who had been peering with brimming eyes through the crack of the closet door, could remain silent no longer.

She rushed frantically across the apartment, seized her hood, and ran from the cottage.

21. Gretel and Hilda

I<small>T WAS RECESS HOUR.</small> At the first stroke of the schoolhouse bell, the canal seemed to give a tremendous
shout and grow suddenly alive with boys and girls.

Dozens of gaily clad children were skating in and
out among each other, and all their pent-up merri-
ment of the morning was relieving itself in song and
shouting and laughter.

At the height of the fun, one of the children called
out:

"What is that?"

"What? Where?" cried a dozen voices.

"Why — don't you see? That dark thing over there
by the idiot's cottage."

"I don't see anything," said one.

"I do," shouted another. "It's a dog!"

"Where's a dog?" put in a squeaky voice. "It's no
such thing — it's a heap of rags."

"Pooh! Voost," retorted another gruffly, "that's
about as near the fact as you ever get. It's the goose-
girl, Gretel."

"Well, what of it?" squeaked Voost. "Isn't she a bundle of rags, I'd like to know?"

"Ha, ha! Pretty good for you, Voost! You'll get a medal for wit yet if you keep on."

"You'd get something else if her brother Hans were here. I'll just bet you would!" said a muffled-up little fellow with a cold in his head.

As Hans was not there, Voost could afford to scoff at the insinuation. "Who cares for him, little sneezer? I'd fight a dozen like him any day, and you in the bargain."

"You would, would you? I'd like to catch you at it," and, by way of proving his words, the sneezer skated off at the top of his speed.

Just then a general chase after three of the biggest boys of the school was proposed, and friend and foe were soon united in a common cause.

Only one of all that happy throng remembered the dark little form by the idiot's cottage. Poor, frightened Gretel! She was not thinking of them, though their merry laughter floated lightly toward her, making her feel like one in a dream.

How loud the moans were behind the darkened window! What if those strange men were really killing her father!

The thought made her spring to her feet with a cry of horror!

"Ah, no," she sobbed, sinking upon the frozen

mound of earth where she had been sitting. "Mother is there, and Hans. They will care for him. But how pale they were. And even Hans was crying!

"Why did the cross old doctor keep him and send me away?" she thought. "I could have clung to the mother and kissed her. That always makes her stroke my hair and speak gently, even after she has scolded me. How quiet it is now! Oh, if the father should die, and Hans, and the mother, what *would* I do?" and Gretel, shivering with cold, buried her face in her arms and cried as if her heart would break.

The poor child had been tasked beyond her strength during the past four days. Through all, she had been her mother's willing little handmaiden, soothing, helping, and cheering the half-widowed woman by day, and watching and praying beside her all the long night. She knew that something terrible and mysterious was taking place at this moment, something that had been too terrible and mysterious for even kind, good Hans to tell.

Then new thoughts came. Why had not Hans told her? It was a shame. It was her father as well as his. She was no baby. She had once taken a sharp knife from the father's hand. She had even drawn him away from the mother on that awful night when Hans, big as he was, could not help her. Why then must she be treated like one who could do nothing? Oh, how very still it was — how bitter, bitter cold! If Annie Bouman

had only stayed home instead of going to Amsterdam,
it wouldn't be so lonely. How cold her feet were
growing — was it the moaning that made her feel as if
she were floating in the air?

This would not do — the mother might need her
help at any moment!

Rousing herself with an effort, Gretel sat upright,
rubbing her eyes and wondering — wondering that
the sky was so bright and blue, wondering at the
stillness in the cottage; wondering, more than all, at
the laughter rising and falling in the distance.

Soon she sank down again, the strange medley of
thought growing more and more confused in her bewildered brain.

What a strange look the doctor had! How the
stork's nest upon the roof seemed to rustle and
whisper down to her! How bright those knives were
in the leathern case — brighter perhaps than the silver
skates. If only she had worn her new jacket, she would
not shiver so. The new jacket was pretty — the only
pretty thing she had ever worn. God had taken care
of her father so long, He would do it still, if those
two men would but go away. Ah, now the meesters
were on the roof; they were clambering to the top —
no, it was her mother and Hans, or the storks — it was
so dark, who could tell? How sweetly the birds were
singing. They must be winter birds, for the air was
thick with icicles — not one bird, but twenty. Oh,

hear them, Mother! Wake me, Mother, for the race — I am so tired from crying and crying . . .

A firm hand was laid upon her shoulder.

"Get up, little girl!" cried a kind voice. "This will not do, for you to lie here and freeze."

Gretel slowly raised her head. She was so sleepy that it did not seem strange to see Hilda van Gleck leaning over her, looking with kind, beautiful eyes into her face. She had often dreamed it before.

But she had never dreamed that Hilda was shaking her roughly, almost dragging her by main force; never dreamed that she heard her saying, "Gretel! Gretel Brinker! you *must* wake!"

This was real. Gretel looked up. Still the lovely, delicate young lady was shaking, rubbing, fairly pounding her. It must be a dream. No, there was the cottage, and the stork's nest, and the meester's coach by the canal. She could see them now quite plainly. Her hands were tingling, her feet throbbing. Hilda was forcing her to walk.

At last Gretel began to feel like herself again.

"I have been asleep," she faltered, rubbing her eyes with both hands.

"Yes indeed, entirely too much asleep," laughed Hilda, whose lips were very pale, "but you are well enough now. Lean upon me, Gretel; there, keep moving — you will soon be warm enough to go in by the fire. Now let me take you into the cottage."

"Oh no, no, no, juffrouw! Not in there! The doctor is there. He sent me away!"

Hilda was puzzled, but she wisely forebore to ask at present for an explanation. "Very well, Gretel, try to walk faster. I saw you on the ground, but I thought you were playing. That is right: keep moving."

All this time the kindhearted girl had been forcing Gretel to walk up and down, supporting her with one arm and, with the other, striving as well as she could to take off her own warm sacque.

Suddenly Gretel suspected her intention.

"Oh juffrouw, juffrouw!" she cried. "*Please* never think of such a thing as *that*. Oh! please keep it on. I am burning all over, juffrouw! I really am burning. Not burning exactly, but pins and needles pricking all over me. Oh, juffrouw, don't!"

The poor child's dismay was so genuine that Hilda hastened to reassure her.

"Very well, Gretel, move your arms then — so. Why, your cheeks are as pink as roses already. I think the doctor would let you in now, he certainly would. Is your father so very ill?"

"Ah, juffrouw," cried Gretel, weeping afresh, "he is dying, I think. There are two doctors in with him at this moment, and the mother has scarce spoken today. Can you hear him moan, juffrouw?" she added, with sudden terror. "The air buzzes so I cannot hear. He may be dead! Oh, I do wish I could hear him!"

Hilda listened. The cottage was very near, but not a sound could be heard. Something told her that Gretel was right. She ran to the window.

"You cannot see there, my lady," Gretel said eagerly. "The mother has oiled paper hanging inside; but at the other one, in the south end of the cottage, you can look in where the paper is torn."

Hilda in her anxiety ran round, past the corner where the low roof was fringed with its loosened thatch.

A sudden thought checked her.

"It is not right for me to peep into another's house in this way," she said to herself; then softly calling to Gretel, she added, in a whisper, "You may look — perhaps he is only sleeping."

Gretel tried to walk briskly toward the spot, but her limbs were trembling. Hilda hastened to her support.

"You are sick yourself, I fear," she said kindly.

"No, not sick, juffrouw, but my heart cries all the time now, even when my eyes are as dry as yours. Why, juffrouw, your eyes are not dry! Are you crying for *us*? Oh, juffrouw, if God sees you! Oh, I know Father will get better now," and Gretel reached up to look through the tiny window.

The sash was sadly patched and broken, a torn piece of paper hung halfway down across it. Gretel's face was pressed to the window.

"Can you see anything?" whispered Hilda at last.

"Yes — the father lies very still, his head is bandaged, and all their eyes are fastened upon him. Oh, juffrouw!" almost screamed Gretel, as she started back, and by a quick, dexterous movement shook off her heavy wooden shoes, "I *must* go in to my mother! Will you come with me?"

"Not now, the bell is ringing. I shall come again soon."

Gretel scarcely heard the words. She remembered for many a day afterward the bright, pitying smile on Hilda's face as she turned away.

22. The Awakening

An ANGEL could not have entered the cottage more noiselessly. Gretel, not daring to look at anyone, slid softly to her mother's side.

The room was very still. She could hear the doctor breathing. She could almost hear the sparks as they fell into the ashes on the hearth. The mother's hand was very cold, but a burning spot glowed on her cheek; and her eyes were like a deer's — so bright, so sad, so eager.

At last there was a movement on the bed, very slight, but enough to cause them all to start. Dr. Boekman leaned eagerly forward. Another movement. The large hand, so white and soft for a poor man's hand, twitched — then raised itself steadily toward the forehead.

It felt the bandage, not in a restless, crazy way, but with a questioning movement that caused even Dr. Boekman to hold his breath. Then the eyes opened slowly.

"Steady! Steady!" said a voice that sounded very strange to Gretel. "Shift that mat higher, boys! Now throw on the clay. The waters are rising fast — no time to . . ."

Dame Brinker sprang forward like a young panther.

She seized his hands, and leaning over him, cried, "Raff! Raff, boy, speak to me!"

"Is it you, Meitje?" he asked faintly. "I have been asleep — hurt, I think. Where is little Hans?"

"Here I am, Father!" shouted Hans, half mad with joy. But the doctor held him back.

"He knows us!" screamed Dame Brinker. "Great God! he knows us! Gretel! Gretel! Come, see your father!"

In vain Dr. Boekman commanded "Silence!" and tried to force them from the bedside. He could not keep them off.

Hans and his mother laughed and cried together, as they hung over the newly awakened man. Gretel made no sound, but gazed at them all with glad, startled eyes. Her father was speaking in a faint voice.

"Is the baby asleep, Meitje?"

"The baby!" echoed Dame Brinker. "Oh, Gretel, that is *you*! And he calls Hans 'little Hans.' Ten years asleep! Oh, mynheer, you have saved us all. He has known nothing for ten years! Children, why don't you thank the meester?"

The good woman was beside herself with joy. Dr. Boekman said nothing, but as his eye met hers he pointed upward. She understood. So did Hans and Gretel.

With one accord they knelt by the cot, side by side. Dame Brinker felt for her husband's hand even while she was praying. Dr. Boekman's head was bowed; the assistant stood by the hearth, his back toward them.

"Why do you pray?" murmured the father, looking feebly from the bed as they rose. "Is it God's day?"

It was not Sunday, but his vrouw bowed her head — she could not speak.

"Then we should have a chapter," said Raff Brinker, speaking slowly and with difficulty. "I do not know how it is. I am very, very weak. Mayhap the minister will read to us."

Gretel lifted the big Dutch Bible from its carved shelf. Dr. Boekman, rather dismayed at being called a minister, coughed and handed the volume to his assistant.

"Read," he muttered. "These people must be kept quiet, or the man will die yet."

When the chapter was finished, Dame Brinker motioned mysteriously to the rest by way of telling them that her husband was asleep.

"Now, juffrouw," said the doctor in a subdued tone, as he drew on his thick woolen mittens, "there must be perfect quiet. You understand. This is truly a most remarkable case. I shall come again tomorrow. Give the patient no food today." And bowing hastily he left the cottage, followed by his assistant.

His grand coach was not far away; the driver had kept the horses moving slowly up and down by the canal all the time the doctor had been in the cottage.

Hans went out also.

"May God bless you, mynheer!" he said, blushing and trembling. "I can never repay you, but if —"

"Yes, you can," interrupted the doctor crossly. "You can use your wits when the patient wakes again. This clacking and sniveling is enough to kill a well man, let alone one lying on the edge of his grave. If you want your father to get well, keep 'em quiet."

So saying, Dr. Boekman, without another word, stalked off to meet his coach, leaving Hans standing there with eyes and mouth wide open.

Hilda was reprimanded severely that day for returning late to school after recess, and for imperfect recitations.

She had remained near the cottage until she heard Dame Brinker laugh, until she had heard Hans say, "Here I am, Father!" and then she had gone back to her lessons. No wonder she missed them! How could she get a long string of Latin verbs by heart when her heart did not care a fig for them, but would keep saying to itself, "Oh, I am so glad! I am so glad!"

Peter, too, was in excellent spirits. He had heard through Hilda of Dame Brinker's laugh and Hans's joyous words, and he needed no further proof that Raff Brinker was a cured man. In fact, the news had gone forth in every direction for miles around. And there was no end to the number of ridiculous stories that were flying about.

Hilda, in the excitement of the moment, had stopped to exchange a word with the doctor's coachman, as he stood by the horses, pommeling his chest and clapping his hands. Her kind heart was overflowing. She could not help pausing to tell the cold, tired-looking man that she thought the doctor would be out soon; she even hinted to him that she suspected — only suspected — that a wonderful cure had been performed: an idiot brought to his senses. Nay, she was *sure* of it, for she had heard his widow laugh — no, not his widow, of course, but his wife — for the man was as much alive as anybody, and for all she knew, sitting up and talking like a lawyer.

All this was very indiscreet. Hilda in an impenitent sort of way felt it to be so.

But it is always so delightful to impart pleasant or surprising news.

She went tripping along by the canal, quite resolved to repeat the sin *ad infinitum,* and tell nearly every girl and boy in the school.

Meanwhile Janzoon Kolp came skating by. Of course, in two seconds he was shouting saucy things to the coachman, who stared at him in disdain.

Janzoon accosted him.

"I say, what's going on at the idiot's cottage? Is your boss in there?"

The coachman nodded mysteriously.

"Whew!" whistled Janzoon, drawing closer. "Old Brinker dead?"

The driver grew big with importance, and silent in proportion.

"Hurry up — what news? Old Brinker dead?" pursued his tormentor.

"No — *cured*! Got his wits," said the coachman, shooting forth his words, one at a time, like so many bullets. Janzoon Kolp jumped as if he had been shot.

Just then he saw a group of boys in the distance. He scampered toward them, forgetting all but the wonderful news.

Therefore, by sundown it was well known throughout the neighboring country that Dr. Boekman, chancing to stop at the cottage, had given the idiot Brinker a tremendous dose of medicine, as brown as gingerbread. It had taken six men to hold him while it was poured down. The idiot had immediately sprung to his feet, in full possession of all his faculties, knocked over the doctor, or thrashed him, then sat down and addressed him for all the world like a lawyer. After that, he had turned and spoken beautifully to his wife and children. Dame Brinker had laughed herself into violent hysterics. Hans had said, "Here I am Father, your own dear son!" and Gretel had said, "Here I am, Father, your own dear Gretel!" and the doctor had afterward been seen leaning back in his carriage looking just as white as a corpse.

23. A New Alarm

WHEN DR. BOEKMAN CALLED the next day at the Brinker cottage, he could not help noticing the cheerful, happy atmosphere of the place. Dame Brinker sat knitting beside the bed, her husband was enjoying a tranquil slumber, and Gretel was noiselessly kneading dark rye bread on the table in the corner.

The doctor did not remain long. He asked a few simple questions, appeared satisfied with the answers, and, after feeling his patient's pulse, said, "Ah, very weak yet, juffrouw, very weak indeed. He must have nourishment. You may begin to feed the patient — ahem! Not too much, but what you do give him let it be strong and of the best."

"Black bread we have, mynheer, and porridge," replied Dame Brinker cheerily; "they have always agreed with him well."

"Tut, tut!" said the doctor, frowning, "nothing of the kind. He must have the juice of fresh meat, white bread, dried and toasted, good Malaga wine, and — ahem! The man looks cold: give him more covering

— something light and warm. Where is the boy?"

"Hans has gone into Broek to look for work. He will be back soon. Will the doctor please be seated?"

Had Dame Brinker's sudden, anxious look of distress frightened the doctor? For he looked hurriedly about him, muttered something about an "extraordinary case," bowed, and disappeared before Dame Brinker had time to say another word.

Gretel frowned, an anxious childish frown, and kneaded the bread dough violently, without looking up. Dame Brinker hurried to her husband's bedside, leaned over him, and fell into silent weeping.

In a moment Hans entered.

"Why, Mother," he whispered in alarm, "what ails thee? Is the father worse?"

She turned her quivering face toward him, making no attempt to conceal her distress.

"He is starving — perishing. The doctor said it."

Hans turned pale.

"What does this mean, Mother? We must feed him at once. Here, Gretel, give me the porridge."

"Nay!" cried his mother distractedly, yet without raising her voice, "it may kill him. Our poor fare is too heavy for him. Oh, Hans, he will die — the father will *die* if we use him this way. He must have meat, and sweet wine, and a dekbed. Oh, what shall I do, what shall I do?" she sobbed, wringing her hands. "There is not a stiver in the house."

Gretel's tears fell one by one into the dough.

"Did the doctor say he *must* have these things, Mother?" asked Hans.

"Yes, he did."

"Well, Mother, don't cry, *he shall have them*; I will bring meat and wine before night. Take the cover from my bed. I can sleep in the straw."

"Yes, Hans; but it is heavy, scant as it is. The doctor said he must have something light and warm. He will perish. Our peat is giving out, Hans."

"Never mind, Mother," whispered Hans cheerfully. "We can cut down the willow tree and burn it, if need be; but I'll bring home something tonight. There must be work in Amsterdam, though there's none in Broek. Never fear, Mother; the worst trouble of all is past. We can brave anything now that the father is himself again."

"Aye," sobbed Dame Brinker hastily drying her eyes, "that is true indeed."

"Of course it is. Look at him, Mother, how softly he sleeps. Do you think God would let him starve, just after giving him back to us? Why, Mother, I'm as sure of getting all the father needs as if my pocket were bursting with gold. There now, don't fret." And hurriedly kissing her, Hans caught up his skates and slipped from the cottage.

Poor Hans! Disappointed not to find work in Broek, half sickened with this new trouble, he tried to whistle as he tramped resolutely off with the firm intention of mending matters.

Want had never before pressed as sorely upon the Brinker family. Their peat was nearly gone, and all the flour in the cottage was in Gretel's dough. They had scarcely cared to eat during the past few days — scarcely realized their condition. Dame Brinker had felt so sure that she and the children could earn money before the worst came that she had given herself up to the joy of her husband's recovery.

Hans reproached himself now that he had not hailed the doctor when he saw him enter his coach and drive rapidly away in the direction of Amsterdam.

"Perhaps there is some mistake," he thought. "The doctor surely would have known that meat and sweet wine were not at our command; and yet the father looks very weak — he certainly does. I *must* get work. If Mynheer van Holp were back from Amsterdam, I could get plenty to do. But Master Peter told me to let him know if he could do aught to serve us. I shall go to him at once. Oh, if only it were summer!"

All this time Hans was hastening toward the canal. Soon his skates were on, and he was skimming rapidly toward the residence of Mynheer van Holp.

"The father must have meat and wine at once," he muttered, "but how can I earn the money in time to buy them today? There is no other way but to go, as I promised, to Master Peter. What would a gift of meat and wine be to him? When the father is once fed, I can rush down to Amsterdam and earn tomorrow's supply."

Then came other thoughts — thoughts that made his heart thump heavily and his cheeks burn with a new shame. "It is *begging,* to say the least. Not one of the Brinkers has ever been a beggar. Shall I be the first? Shall my poor father, just coming back into life, learn that his family has begged for charity — he, always so wise and thrifty? No," cried Hans aloud, "better a thousand times to part with the watch.

"I can at least borrow money on it in Amsterdam," he thought, turning around. "That will be no disgrace. I can find work at once and get it back again. Nay, perhaps I can even speak to the father about it!"

This last thought made his heart leap for joy. Why not, indeed, speak to the father? He was a rational being now. "He may wake," thought Hans, "quite bright and rested — may tell us the watch is of no consequence, and to sell it of course! Huzza!" and Hans almost flew over the ice.

A few moments more, and the skates were again swinging from his arm. He was running toward the cottage. His mother met him at the door.

"Oh, Hans!" she cried, her face radiant with joy, "the young lady has been here with her maid. She brought everything — meat, jelly, wine, and bread — a whole basketful! Then the doctor sent a man from town with more wine, and a fine bed and blankets for the father. Oh, he will get well now. God bless them!"

"God bless them!" echoed Hans, and for the first time that day his eyes filled with tears.

24. The Father's Return

THAT EVENING Raff Brinker felt so much better that he insisted upon sitting up a while on the rough, high-backed chair by the fire. For a few moments there was quite a commotion in the little cottage. Hans was all-important on the occasion, for his father was a heavy man, and needed someone strong to lean upon. The dame was in such a state of alarm and excitement at the bold step they were taking — lifting him without the doctor's orders — that she came near pulling her husband over.

"Steady, vrouw, steady," panted Raff. "Have I grown old and feeble, or is it the fever makes me thus helpless?"

"Hear the man!" laughed Dame Brinker. "Why, you're only weak from the fever, Raff. Here's the chair, all fixed snug and warm; now, sit thee down — hi-d-didy — there we are!"

With these words, Dame Brinker let her half of the burden settle slowly into the chair, and Hans did the same.

147

Meanwhile Gretel flew about bringing every possible thing to her mother to tuck behind the father's back and spread over his knees.

The father was "sitting up" at last. What wonder that he looked about him like one bewildered? "Little Hans" had just been almost carrying him. "The baby" was over four feet tall, and was demurely brushing up the hearth with a bundle of willow wisps. Meitje, the vrouw, winsome and fair as ever, had gained at least twenty pounds in what seemed to him a few hours. The only familiar things in the room were the pine table that he had made before he was married, the Bible upon the shelf, and the cupboard in the corner.

It was only natural that Raff Brinker's eyes filled with hot tears even while looking at the joyful faces of his loved ones. Ten years dropped from a man's life are no small loss: ten years of manhood, of household happiness and care; ten years of honest labor, of enjoying the sunshine and outdoor beauty; ten years of grateful life — one day looking forward to all this, the next waking to find them passed and a blank. What wonder the scalding tears dropped one by one upon his cheek!

Tender little Gretel! The prayer of her life was answered through those tears. She loved her father from that moment. Hans and his mother glanced silently at each other when they saw her spring toward him and throw her arms about his neck.

"Father, *dear* Father," she whispered, pressing her

cheek close to his, "don't cry. We are all here."

"God bless thee," sobbed Raff, kissing her, "I had forgotten that!"

Soon he looked up again, and spoke in a cheerful voice. "I should know her, vrouw," he said, holding the sweet young face between his hands, and gazing at it as though he were watching it grow. "I should know her. The same blue eyes, and the lips, and, ah me, the little song she could sing almost before she could stand. But that was long ago," he added, with a sigh, still looking at her dreamily, "long ago; it's all gone now."

"Not so, indeed," cried Dame Brinker eagerly. "Do you think I would let her forget it? Gretel, child, sing the old song thou hast known so long!"

Raff Brinker's hands fell wearily and his eyes closed, but it was something to see the smile playing about his mouth as Gretel's voice floated about him like an incense.

It was a simple air; she had never known the words.

With loving instinct she softened every note, until Raff almost fancied that his two-year-old baby was once more beside him.

As soon as the song was finished, Hans climbed up on the stool and began to rummage in the cupboard. Then jumping down, he walked toward his father and placed an oblong block of pine wood in his hands. One of its ends was rounded off, and some deep cuts had been made on the top.

"Do you know what it is, Father?" asked Hans.

Raff Brinker's face brightened. "Indeed, I do, boy! It is the boat I was making you yest— Alack, not yesterday, but years ago."

"I have kept it ever since, Father; it can be finished when your hand grows strong again."

"Yes, but not for you, my lad. I must wait for the grandchildren. Why, you are nearly a man. Have you helped your mother, boy, through all these years?"

"Aye, and bravely," put in Dame Brinker.

"Let me see," muttered the father, looking in a puzzled way at them all, "how long is it since the night when the waters were coming in? 'Tis the last I remember."

"We have told thee true, Raff. It was ten years ago."

"Ten years — and I fell then, you say. Has the fever been on me ever since?"

Dame Brinker scarcely knew how to reply. The doctor had charged her on no account to worry or excite his patient.

"Like enough, Raff," she said, nodding her head and raising her eyebrows. "When a heavy man like thee falls on his head, it's hard to say what will come. But thou'rt well *now*, Raff. Thank the good Lord!"

The newly awakened man bowed his head.

"Aye, well enough, mine vrouw," he said, after a moment's silence, "but it will not be right till I get on the dykes again. When shall I be at work, think you?"

"Hear the man!" cried Dame Brinker, delighted, yet frightened too. "We must get him on the bed, Hans. Work, indeed!"

They tried to raise him from the chair, but he was not ready yet.

"Be off with ye!" he said, with something like his old smile. "Does a man want to be lifted about like a log? I tell you, before three suns I shall be on the dykes again. Ah, there'll be some stout fellows to greet me! Jan Kamphuisen and young Hoogvliet. They have been good friends to thee, Hans, I'll warrant."

Hans looked at his mother. Young Hoogsvliet had been dead five years. Jan Kamphuisen was in the jail at Amsterdam.

"Aye, they'd have done their share, no doubt," said Dame Brinker, parrying the inquiry, "had we asked them. But what with working and studying, Hans has been busy enough without seeking comrades."

"Working and studying," echoed Raff, in a musing tone. "Can the youngsters read and cipher, Meitje?"

"You should hear them!" she answered proudly. "They can run through a book while I mop the floor. And as for ciphering —"

"Here, lad, help a bit," interrupted Raff Brinker. "I must get me on the bed again."

25. The Thousand Guilders

NONE SEEING THE HUMBLE SUPPER eaten in the Brinker cottage that night would have dreamed of the dainty fare hidden away nearby. Hans and Gretel looked rather wistfully toward the cupboard, but even in thought they did not rob their father.

"He relished his supper well," said Dame Brinker, nodding sidewise toward the bed, "and fell asleep the next moment. Ah, the dear man will be feeble for many a day. He wanted to sit up again, but while I made a show of humoring him and getting ready, he dropped off — what, Hans, dreaming?"

"Oh no, Mother, I was only thinking —"

"Thinking, about what? Ah, no use asking," she added in a changed tone. "I was thinking of the same a while ago. Well, well, it's no blame if we did look to hear something by this time about the thousand guilders; but not a word."

Hans looked up anxiously, dreading lest his mother should grow agitated, as usual, when speaking of the lost money; but she was staring toward the window.

"Thousand guilders," echoed a faint voice from the bed. "Ah, I am sure they have been of good use to you, vrouw, through the long years while your man was idle."

The poor woman started up. "Are you awake, Raff?" she faltered.

"Yes, Meitje, and I feel much better. Our money was well saved, vrouw, I was saying. Did it last through all these ten years?"

"I — I — have not got it, Raff. I —" She was going to tell him the whole truth, when Hans lifted his finger warningly and whispered, "Remember what the doctor told us: the father must not be worried."

"Speak to him, child," she answered, trembling.

Hans hurried to the bedside.

"I am glad you are feeling better," he said, leaning over his father. "Another day will see you quite strong again."

"Aye, like enough. How long did the money last, Hans? I could not hear what your mother said."

"I said, Raff," stammered Dame Brinker in great distress, "that it was all gone."

"Well, well, wife, do not fret at that. One thousand guilders is not so very much for ten years, and with children to bring up; but it has helped to make you all comfortable. Have you had much sickness to bear?"

"N-no," sobbed Dame Brinker, lifting her apron to her eyes.

"Tut-tut, woman, why do you cry?" said Raff kindly. "We will soon fill another pouch, when I am on my feet again. Lucky I told you all about it before I fell."

"Told me what, man?"

"Why, that I buried the money. In my dream just now, it seemed I had never said aught about it."

Dame Brinker started forward. Hans caught her arm. "Hist! Mother," he whispered, hastily leading her away, "we must be very careful." Then, while she stood with clasped hands waiting in breathless anxiety, he once more approached the cot. Trembling with eagerness, he said, "That was a troublesome dream. Do you remember *when* you buried the money, Father?"

"Yes, my boy. It was before daylight on the same day I was hurt. Jan Kampuisen said something the sundown before that made me distrust his honesty. He was the only one living besides your mother who knew we had saved a thousand guilders, so I rose up that night and buried the money — blockhead that I was, ever to suspect an old friend!"

"I'll be bound, Father," pursued Hans in a laughing voice, motioning to his mother and Gretel to remain quiet, "that you've forgotten where you buried it."

"Ha, ha! Not I, indeed. But good night, my son, I can sleep again."

Hans would have walked away, but his mother's gestures were not to be disobeyed, so he said gently,

"Good night, Father. Where did you say you buried the money? I was only a little one then."

"Close by the willow sapling behind the cottage," said Raff Brinker drowsily.

"Ah, yes. North side of the tree, wasn't it, Father?"

"No, the south side. Now, son, easy; shift this pillow — so. Good night."

"Good night, Father!" said Hans, ready to dance for joy.

The moon rose very late that night, shining in full and clear at the little window, but its beams did not disturb Raff Brinker. He slept soundly, and so did Gretel. But Hans and his mother had things to do.

After making a few hurried preparations, they stole forth with bright, expectant faces, bearing a broken spade and a rusty implement Raff had used when he worked on the dykes. It was so light out of doors that they could see the willow tree distinctly. The frozen ground was hard as stone, but Hans and his mother were resolute. Their only dread was that they might disturb the sleepers in the cottage.

"This icebreaker is just the thing, Mother," said Hans, striking many a vigorous blow, "but the ground has set so firm, it'll be a fair match for it."

"Never fear, Hans," she answered, watching him eagerly. "Here, let me try a while."

They soon succeeded in making an impression; one opening, and the rest was not so difficult.

Still they worked on. Now and then Dame Brinker

stepped noiselessly over the threshold and listened, to be certain that her husband slept.

"What grand news it will be for him," she said, laughing. "How I should like to put the pouch and the stocking, just as we find them, all full of money, near him this blessed night, for the dear man to see when he wakens."

"We must get them first, Mother," panted Hans, digging away.

"There's no doubt of that. They can't slip away from us now," she answered, shivering with cold and excitement. "Like enough we'll find them stowed in the old earthen pot I lost long ago."

By this time Hans, too, began to tremble, but not with cold. He had penetrated a foot deep for quite a space on the south side of the tree.

"Strange that the dear father should have put it down so woeful deep," said Dame Brinker. "Ah, the ground was soft enough then, I warrant. How wise of him to mistrust Jan Kamphuisen. Now, Hans, let me take a turn."

Hour after hour, mother and son worked on. The hole grew larger and deeper. Not until moon and stars faded away and streaks of daylight began to appear did Meitje Brinker and Hans look hopelessly into each other's face.

They had searched thoroughly, desperately, all round the tree: south, north, east, west. *The hidden money was not there!*

26. Glimpses

Annie Bouman had a healthy distaste for Janzoon Kolp, and could not, "to save her life," say one civil word to that "odious" boy. Of course they were thrown together very often, and while Annie detested him more and more, Janzoon liked her better every day.

"Janzoon Kolp, you impudent boy, go away," Annie often said. "I don't want your company."

"Ha, ha!" Janzoon would laugh to himself. "Girls never say what they mean. I'll skate with her every chance I get."

And so the pretty maid would not look up that morning when, skating homeward from Amsterdam, she noticed a great burly boy, much like Janzoon, coming down the canal toward her.

"Humph! If I look at him," thought Annie, "I'll —"

"Good morrow, Annie Bouman," she heard a pleasant voice say.

[How a smile brightens a girl's face!]

"Good morrow, Master Hans, I am right glad to meet you."

[How a smile brightens a boy's face!]

"Annie, there has been a great change at our house since you left."

"How so?" she exclaimed, opening her eyes very wide.

Hans, who had been in a great hurry, now grew talkative and quite at leisure in Annie's sunshine. Turning about, and skating slowly with her toward Broek, he told the good news of his father. Annie was so true a friend that he told her even of how money was needed, and how everything depended upon his obtaining work, but that he could find nothing to do in the neighborhood.

All this was said not as a complaint, but because she was looking at him and wished to know. He could not speak of last night's bitter disappointment, for that was a secret.

"Good-bye, Annie," he said at last. "The morning is going fast, and I must hasten to Amsterdam to sell these skates. Mother must have money at once. Before nightfall I shall certainly find a job somewhere."

"Sell your new skates, Hans!" cried Annie. "You, the best skater around Broek. Why, the race is coming off in five days."

"I know it," he answered resolutely. "Good-bye. I shall skate home again on the old wooden ones —" and Hans was off like an arrow.

"Hans, come back!" she called.

Her voice changed the "arrow" into a top. Spinning around, he darted, in one long, leaning sweep, toward her.

"Then you really are going to sell your new skates?"

"Of course I am," he replied, looking up with a surprised smile.

"Well, Hans, if you *are* going to sell your skates," said Annie, "I mean — well, I know somebody who would like to buy them, that's all. You won't get half the price for them in Amsterdam. *Please* give them to me. I'll bring you the money this very afternoon."

"Annie," he said, taking off the skates and handing them to her, "I am sorry to be so particular, but if your friend should not want them, will you bring them back to me today? I must buy peat and meal for the mother early tomorrow morning."

"My friend will want them," laughed Annie, nodding gaily and skating off at top speed.

As Hans drew forth the old wooden skates from his capacious pockets and fastened them on, he did not hear Annie murmur, "I wish I had not been so pert — poor, brave Hans." And as Annie skated homeward filled with pleasant thoughts, she did not hear Hans say, "I grumbled like a bear. But bless her! some girls are like angels!"

27. Looking for Work

THE WOODEN RUNNERS squeaked more than ever. It was as much as Hans could do to get on with the clumsy old things, but he resolutely pushed back the regret that he had not been able to keep the beautiful skates just a little longer — at least until after the race.

"Mother surely will not be angry with me," he thought, "for selling them without her leave. It will be full time to speak of it when I take home the money."

Hans went up and down the streets of Amsterdam that day, looking for work. He earned a few stivers by assisting a man in driving a train of loaded mules into the city, but he could not find steady employment anywhere. He would have been glad to work as porter or errand boy, but there was no place for him. Some of the shopkeepers said they had just hired someone. Others merely shook their heads at him.

At the factories, he met with no better luck. It seemed to him that in those great buildings, turning out such tremendous quantities of woolens, cottons, and linens, such dyes and paints, and bricks, glass, and china — that in at least one of these, a strong-armed boy, able and eager to work, could find something to do. But no — the same answer met him everywhere: "No." If he had called before Saint Nicholas' Day they might have given him a job — they were hurried then — but at present they had more boys than they needed.

Hans did not know how much anxiety showed in his eyes, and how, more than once, the gruffest denials were given with the uncomfortable thought that this lad ought not to be turned away. And before morning one man actually resolved that if the Broek boy came in again he would instruct his head man to set him at something. But Hans knew nothing of all this.

Toward sundown he started back to Broek. There was one more chance: Mynheer van Holp might have returned by this time. Master Peter, it was reported, had gone to Amsterdam the night before to attend to something connected with the great skating race. Still, Hans would go and try.

Fortunately, Peter had returned early that morning. He was at home when Hans reached there, and was just about to start for the Brinker cottage.

"Ah, Hans!" he cried as the weary boy approached the door. "You are the very one I wish to see. Come in and warm yourself."

Hans left the van Holp mansion with a lightened heart. Peter had brought word from his father that young Brinker was to commence working upon the summerhouse doors immediately. There was a comfortable, well-equipped workshop on the place, and it was to be at his service until the carving was done.

Peter did not tell Hans that he had skated all the way to Haarlem for the purpose of arranging this plan with Mynheer van Holp. It was enough for him to see the glad, eager look on young Brinker's face.

"I think I can do it," said Hans, "though I have never learned the trade."

"I am sure you can," responded Peter heartily. "How is your father today?"

"Better, mynheer — he improves every hour."

"It is the most astonishing thing I ever heard of. That gruff doctor is a great fellow after all."

"Ah, mynheer," said Hans warmly, "he is more than great. He is good. But for the doctor's kind heart and great skill, my poor father would yet be in the dark. I think, mynheer," he added, with kindling eyes, "surgery is the very noblest science in the world."

Peter shrugged his shoulders. "Very noble it may be, but not quite to my taste. This Dr. Boekman certainly has skill, but defend me from such hearts as his!"

"Why do you say so, mynheer?" asked Hans.

Just then a lady slowly entered from an adjoining

apartment. It was Mevrouw van Holp arrayed in the
grandest of caps and the longest of satin aprons. She
nodded placidly as Hans stepped back from the fire
and bowed.

Peter at once drew a high-backed oaken chair toward the fire, and the lady seated herself. Hans
turned to go.

"Wait a moment, if you please, young man," said
the lady. "I accidentally overheard you and my son
speaking of my friend Dr. Boekman. You are right:
Dr. Boekman has a very kind heart. You perceive,
Peter, we may be quite mistaken in judging a person
solely by his manners, though courtesy is not to be
despised."

"I intended no disrespect, Mother," said Peter,
"but surely one has no right to go growling through
the world."

"Ah, Peter, Surgeon Boekman has had a great sor-
row. Many years ago he lost his only child, a fine lad,
under very painful circumstances. Before then,
Gerard Boekman was one of the most agreeable
gentlemen I ever knew."

So saying, Mevrouw van Holp, looking kindly upon
the two boys, arose and left the room.

Peter, only half convinced, conducted his visitor to
the door. Before they parted, he advised Hans to
keep himself in good skating order, "for," he added,
"now that your father is all right, you will be in fine
spirits for the race. That will be the best skating show

ever seen in this part of the world — everybody is talking of it. You are to try for the prize, remember."

"I shall not be in the race, mynheer," said Hans, looking down.

"Not be in the race! Why not, indeed?" and immediately Peter's thoughts swept on a full tide of suspicion toward Carl Schummel.

"Because I cannot, mynheer," answered Hans, as he bent to slip his feet into his big shoes.

Something in the boy's manner warned Peter not to press the matter further. He bade Hans good-bye, and stood thoughtfully watching him as he walked away.

In a minute Peter called out, "Hans Brinker!"

"Yes, mynheer."

"I'll take back all I said about Dr. Boekman."

"Yes, mynheer."

Both were laughing. But Peter's smile changed to a look of puzzled surprise when he saw Hans kneel down by the canal and put on the wooden skates.

"Very queer," muttered Peter, shaking his head. "Why in the world doesn't Hans wear his new ones?"

28. The Fairy Godmother

THE SUN HAD GONE DOWN when Hans jerked off the wooden runners and trudged hopefully toward the Brinker cottage. Two slight figures were moving past it.

That gray, well-patched jacket, that dull blue skirt and apron, that faded close-fitting cap, and those quick little feet in their great boatlike wooden shoes — they were Gretel's of course.

That bright red jacket and pretty skirt, that graceful cap bobbing over the gold earring, that dainty apron, and those snug leather shoes that seemed to have grown with the feet — why Hans could have sworn they were Annie's.

The two girls were slowly pacing up and down in front of the cottage. Their arms were entwined, and their heads were nodding and shaking emphatically.

With a joyous shout, Hans hastened toward them. "Gretel! Annie! I've found work!"

This brought his mother to the cottage door.

She, too, had pleasant tidings. The father was still improving. He had been sitting up nearly all day, and was now sleeping, "just as quiet as a lamb."

"It is my turn for news now, Hans," said Annie, drawing him aside after he had told his mother the good word from Mynheer van Holp. "Your skates are sold, and here's the money."

"Seven guilders!" cried Hans, counting the pieces in astonishment. "Why, that is three times as much as I paid for them."

"I cannot help that," said Annie. "If the buyer knew no better, it is not our fault."

Hans looked up quickly.

"Oh, Annie!"

"Oh, Hans!" she mimicked, pursing her lips.

"Now, Annie, I know you would never mean that! You must return some of this money."

"But I'll do no such thing," insisted Annie. "They're sold, and that's an end of it." Then seeing that he looked really pained, she added in a lower tone, "Will you believe me, Hans, when I say that there has been no mistake — that the person who bought your skates *insisted* upon paying seven guilders for them?"

"I will," he answered, and the light from his clear blue eyes seemed to settle and sparkle under Annie's lashes.

Dame Brinker was delighted at the sight of the silver, but when she learned that Hans had parted with his treasures to obtain it, she sighed, as she exclaimed, "Bless thee, child! That will be a sore loss for thee!"

"Here, Mother," said the boy, plunging his hands far into his pockets, "here is more — we shall be rich if we keep on!"

"Aye, indeed," she answered. Then, lowering her voice, she added. "We *would* be rich but for that Jan Kamphuisen. He was at the willow tree years ago, Hans — depend upon it!"

"Indeed, it seems likely," sighed Hans. "Well, Mother, we must give up the money bravely. It is certainly gone. Let us think no more about it."

"That's easy saying, Hans. I shall try, but it's hard, and my poor man wanting so many comforts. Bless me! The girls were here but this instant. Where did they run to?"

"They slipped behind the cottage," said Hans, "like enough to hide from us. Hist! I'll catch them for you. They both move quicker than yonder rabbit."

"Why, there *is* a rabbit. Hold, Hans, the poor thing must have been in sore need to venture from its burrow this bitter weather. I'll get a few crumbs for it."

The good woman bustled into the cottage. Soon she came out again, but Hans had forgotten to wait, and the rabbit was gone. Turning the corner of the cottage, Dame Brinker came upon the children. Hans and Gretel were standing before Annie, who was seated carelessly upon a stump.

"That is a good as a picture!" cried Dame Brinker, halting in admiration of the group. "Annie, you look like a fairy."

"Do I?" laughed Annie, sparkling with animation. "Well then, Gretel and Hans, imagine I'm your godmother just paying you a visit. Now I'll grant you each a wish. What will thou have, Master Hans?"

A shade of earnestness passed over Annie's face as she looked up at him, as if she wished that for once she could have a fairy's power.

To Hans, at that moment, she seemed more than mortal.

"I wish," said he solemnly, "I could find something I was searching for last night."

Gretel laughed merrily. Dame Brinker moaned, "Shame on you, Hans!" and passed wearily into the cottage.

The fairy godmother sprang up and stamped her foot three times.

"Thou shalt have thy wish," said she. Then, with playful solemnity, she put her hand in her apron pocket and drew forth a large glass bead. "Bury this," said she, giving it to Hans, "where I have stamped, and ere moonrise thy wish shall be granted."

Gretel laughed more merrily than ever.

The godmother pretended great displeasure.

"Naughty child," said she, scowling terribly. "In punishment for laughing at a fairy, *thy* wish shall *not* be granted."

"Ha!" cried Gretel in high glee, "Better wait till you're asked, godmother. I haven't made any wish!"

Annie acted her part well. Never smiling through all their merry laughter, she stalked away, all offended dignity.

"Good night, fairy!" they cried.

"Good night, mortals!" Annie called out at last as she sprang over a frozen ditch and ran quickly homeward.

"Oh, isn't she — just like a flower — so sweet and lovely!" cried Gretel, looking after her in great admiration. Why, Hans! What are you going to do?"

"Wait and see!" answered Hans as he plunged into the cottage and came out again, all in an instant, bearing the spade and icebreaker in his hands. "I'm going to bury my magic bead!"

Raff Brinker still slept soundly; his wife took a small block of peat and put it on the embers. Then opening the door, she called gently:

"Come in, children."

"Mother! Mother! See here!" shouted Hans.

"Holy Saint Bavon!" exclaimed the dame, springing over the doorstep. "What ails the boy!"

"Come quick, Mother," he cried, in great excitement, working with all his might and driving in the icebreaker at each word. "Don't you see? *This* is the spot — right here on the south side of the stump. Why didn't we think of it last night? The *stump* is the old willow tree — the one you cut down last spring because it shaded the potatoes. That little tree wasn't here!"

Dame Brinker could not speak. She dropped on her knees beside Hans just in time to see him drag forth — *the old stone pot!*

He thrust in his hand and took out the stocking and the pouch, black and moldy, but filled with the long-lost treasure!

Such a time! Such laughing! Such crying! Such counting, after they went into the cottage! It was a wonder that Raff did not waken. His dreams were pleasant, however, for he smiled in his sleep.

Dame Brinker and her children had a fine supper — no need to save the delicacies now.

"We'll get Father some nice fresh things tomorrow," said the dame, as she brought forth cold meat, wine, bread, and jelly, and placed them on the clean pine table. "Sit by, children, sit by."

29. The Mysterious Watch

SOMETHING ELSE WAS BROUGHT TO LIGHT on the day the missing guilders were found. This was the story of the watch that for ten long years had been so jealously guarded by Raff's faithful vrouw. Many a time she had dreaded to look on it, lest she be tempted to disobey her husband's request. It had been hard to see her children hungry and to know that the watch, if sold, would bring roses to their cheeks again. "But nay," she would exclaim, "Meitje Brinker is not one to forget her man's last bidding, come what may."

"Take good care of this, mine vrouw," he had said, as he handed it to her—that was all. No explanation followed, for just then a workman had rushed into the cottage, crying, "Come, man! The waters are rising! You're wanted on the dykes."

Raff had started at once, and that was the last she had seen of him in his right mind.

On the day when Hans was in Amsterdam looking for work, and Gretel, after performing her household labors, was wandering about in search of chips, twigs

— anything to use for fuel — Dame Brinker with suppressed excitement had laid the watch in her husband's hand.

"It wasn't in reason," as she afterward said to Hans, "to wait any longer, when a word from the father would settle all; no woman living but would want to know how he came by that watch."

Raff Brinker turned the bright, polished thing over and over in his hand, then examined the bit of smoothly ironed black ribbon fastened to it — he seemed hardly to recognize it. At last he said, "Ah, I remember this! Why, you've been rubbing it, vrouw, till it shines like a new guilder."

"Aye," said Dame Brinker, nodding her head complacently.

Raff looked at it again. "Poor boy!" he murmured, then fell into a brown study.

This was too much for the dame. "Poor boy!" she echoed. "What do you think I'm standing here for, Raff Brinker, and my spinning awaiting, if not to hear more than that?"

"I told ye all, long since," said Raff positively, as he looked up in surprise.

"Indeed, and you never did!" retorted the vrouw.

"Well, if not, since it's no affair of ours, we'll say no more about it," said Raff, shaking his head sadly. "Like enough while I've been dead on the earth all this time, the poor boy's died and been in heaven. He looked near enough to it, poor lad!"

"Raff Brinker! If you're going to treat me this way, and I nursing you and bearing with you since I was twenty-two years old, it's a shame," cried the vrouw, growing quite red and scant of breath.

Raff's voice was feeble yet. "Treat you what way, Meitje?"

" 'What way!' " said Dame Brinker, mimicking his voice and manner, "what way? Why, just as every woman in the world is treated after she's stood by a man through the worst, like —"

"Meitje!"

Raff was leaning forward, with outstretched arms. His eyes were full of tears.

In an instant Dame Brinker was at his feet, clasping his hands in hers.

"Oh, what have I done! Made my good man cry, and he not back with me four days! Look up, Raff! Nay, Raff, my own boy, I'm sorry I hurt thee. It's hard not to be told about the watch after waiting ten years to know; but I'll ask thee no more, Raff. Here, we'll put the thing away that's made the first trouble between us, after God just giving thee back to me."

"I was a fool to cry, Meitje," he said, kissing her, "and it's no more than right ye should know the truth. But it seemed like it might be telling the secrets of the dead to talk about the matter."

"Is the man — the lad — thou wert talking of, dead, think thee?" asked the vrouw.

"It's hard telling," he answered.

"Was he so sick, Raff?"

"No, not sick, I may say; but troubled, vrouw, very troubled."

"Had he done any wrong, think ye?" she asked, lowering her voice.

Raff nodded.

"*Murder?*" whispered the wife, not daring to look up.

"He said it was like to that, indeed."

"Oh, Raff, you frighten me! You speak so strange, and you tremble. I must know all."

"If I tremble, mine vrouw, it must be from the fever. There is no guilt on my soul, thank God!"

"Take a sip of this wine, Raff. There — now you are better. It was like a crime, you were saying."

"Aye, Meitje, like to murder — *that* he told me himself. But I'll never believe it. A likely lad, fresh and honest-looking as our own youngster, but with something not so bold and straight about him."

"Aye, I know," said the dame gently, fearing to interrupt the story.

"He came upon me quite sudden," continued Raff, "the palest, frightenedest face that ever was. He caught me by the arm. 'You look like an honest man,' says he."

"Aye, he was right in that," interrupted the dame emphatically.

Raff looked somewhat bewildered.

"Where was I, my vrouw?"

"The lad took hold of your arm, Raff," she said, gazing at him anxiously.

"Aye, so. The words come awkward to me, and everything is half like a dream, ye see."

"What wonder, poor man," sighed the dame, stroking his hand. "If ye had not head enough for a dozen, the wit would never have come to ye again. Well, the lad caught ye by the arm and said ye looked honest. What then? Was it noontime?"

"Nay; before daylight — long before early chimes."

"It was the same day you were hurt," said the dame. "I know it seemed you went to your work in the middle of the night. You left off where he caught your arm, Raff."

"Yes," resumed her husband; "and I can see his face this minute — so white and wild-looking. 'Take me down the river a way,' says he. I was working then, you'll remember, far down on the line, across from Amsterdam. I told him I was no boatman. 'It's an affair of life and death,' says he. 'Take me on a few miles — yonder skiff is not locked, but it may be a poor man's boat, and I'd be loath to rob him!' Well, I took him down, it might be six or eight miles, and then he said he could run the rest of the way on shore. I was in haste to get the boat back. Before he jumped out, he says, sobbing-like, 'I can trust you. I've done a thing — God knows I never intended it — the man is dead. I must fly from Holland.'"

"What was it, did he say, Raff? Had he been shooting at a comrade, like they do down at the University of Göttingen?"

"I can't recall that. Mayhap he told me, but it's all like a dream. I said it wasn't for me, a good Hollander, to cheat the laws of my country by helping him off that way; but he kept saying, 'God knows I am innocent!' and looked at me in the starlight as fair now and clear-eyed as our Hans might — and I just pulled away faster."

"It must have been Jan Kamphuisen's boat," remarked Dame Brinker dryly. "None other would have left his oars out that careless."

"Aye, it was Jan's boat, sure enough. The man will be coming in to see me Sunday, likely, if he's heard; and young Hoogsvliet, too. Where was I?"

"Where were you? Why, not far, forsooth — the lad hadn't yet given ye the watch. Alack, I misgive whether he came by it honestly!"

"Why, vrouw," exclaimed Raff in an injured tone, "he was dressed soft and fine as the prince himself. The watch was his own, clear enough."

"How came he to give it up?" asked the dame.

"I told ye just now," he answered, with a puzzled air.

"Tell me again," said Dame Brinker, wisely warding off another digression.

"Well, just before jumping from the boat, he says, handing me the watch, 'I'm flying from my country as I never thought I could. I'll trust you because you look honest. Will you take this to my father — not to-day but in a week, and tell him his unhappy boy sent it; and tell him if ever the time comes that he wants me to come back to him, I'll brave everything and come. Tell him to send a letter to — to — there, the rest is all gone from me. I can't remember where the letter was to go. Poor lad!" resumed Raff, sorrowfully tak-ing the watch from his vrouw's lap, as he spoke. "And it's never never been sent to his father to this day."

"I'll take it, Raff, never fear — the moment Gretel gets back. She will be in soon. What was the father's name, did you say? Where were you to find him?"

"Alack!" answered Raff, speaking very slowly, "it's slipped my mind. I can see the lad's face, and his great eyes, just as plain — and I remember his opening the watch and snatching something from it and kissing it, but no more."

"Aye, Raff. You're tired now — I must get ye straight on the bed again. Where is the child, I wonder?"

Dame Brinker opened the door, and called, "Gretel! Gretel!"

"Stand aside, vrouw," said Raff, feebly, as he leaned forward and endeavored to look out upon the bare landscape. "I've half a mind to stand beyond the door just once."

"Nay, nay," she laughed, "I'll tell the doctor how ye tease and fidget and bother to be let out in the air, and if he says you can, I'll bundle ye warm tomorrow and give ye a turn on your feet. But I'm freezing you with this door open. I declare if there isn't Gretel with her apron full, skating on the canal like wild. Why, man," she continued almost in a scream, as she slammed the door, "thou'rt walking to the bed without my touching thee! Thou'lt fall!"

The dame's loving tone showed her mingled fear and delight, even more than the rush she made toward her husband. Soon he was comfortably settled under the new cover, declaring, as his vrouw tucked him in snug and warm, that it was the last daylight that should see him abed.

"Aye! I can hope it myself," laughed Dame Brinker, "now you have been frisking about at this rate." As Raff closed his eyes, the dame hastened to revive the fire. Then, putting her spinning wheel away, she drew forth her knitting from some invisible pocket and seated herself by the bedside.

"If you could remember that man's name, Raff," she began cautiously, "I might take the watch to him while you're sleeping; Gretel will be in soon."

Raff tried to think, but in vain.

"Could it be Boomphoffen?" suggested the dame. "I've heard how they've had two sons turn out bad: Gerard and Lambert."

"It might be," said Raff. "Look if there's letters on the watch; that'll guide us some."

"Bless thee, man," cried the happy dame, eagerly lifting the watch, "why thou'rt sharper than ever!

Sure enough. Here's letters! L.J.B.! That's Lambert
Boomphoffen, you may depend. What the J is for I
can't say; but they used to be very grand people,
just the kind to give their children all double names."

"I don't know but you've got the right guess at a
jump, vrouw. It was your way always," said Raff,
closing his eyes. "Take the watch to Boompkinks and
try."

"Not Boompkinks, I know no such name; it's
Boomphoffen."

"Aye, take it there."

"Take it there, man! Why, the whole brood of 'em's
been gone to America these four years. But go to sleep,
Raff; it'll come to you, what's best to do, in the
morning.

"So Mistress Gretel! Here you are at last!"

Before Raff awoke that evening, the fairy godmother Annie had been to the cottage, the guilders
were once more safely locked in the big chest, and
Dame Brinker and the children were faring sump-
tuously on meat and white bread and wine.

So the mother, in the joy of her heart, told them the
story of the watch.

30. A Discovery

THE NEXT DAY, the news of the thousand guilders had, of course, to be told to the father. Such tidings as that surely could not harm him. Then while Gretel was diligently obeying her mother's injunction to "clean the place fresh as new," Hans and the dame sallied forth to purchase peat and provisions.

Hans was carefree and contented. The dame was filled with delightful new anxieties — suddenly, there were ten thousand guilders' worth of new wants. The happy woman talked of them so freely to Hans on their way to Amsterdam, and brought back such little bundles after all, that he scratched his bewildered head as he leaned against the chimney piece, wondering whether, "bigger the purse, tighter the string."

"What thinking on, Big Eyes?" chirruped his mother, half reading his thoughts as she bustled about, preparing the dinner. "What thinking on? Ye'll grow to the chimney place with your staring and wondering.

"Now, Raff, here's your chair at the head of the table, where it should be, for there's a man to the house now — aye, that's the way — lean on Hans; there's a strong staff for you! Sit by, my man, sit by."

"Can you call to mind, vrouw," said Raff, settling himself cautiously in the chair, "the wonderful music box that cheered your working in the big house at Heidelberg when you were a girl?"

"Aye, that I can," answered the dame, "three turns of a brass key, and the witchy thing would send the music fairly running up and down one's back. I remember it well. But, Raff, you would never throw our guilders away for a thing like that?"

"No, no, not I, vrouw; for the good Lord has already given me a music box without pay."

All three cast quick, frightened glances at one another and at Raff. Were his wits on the wing again?

"Aye, a music box," insisted Raff. "It's set going by the turn of a mop handle, and it slips and glides around the room, carrying the music about till you'd swear the birds were back again."

"Holy Saint Bavon!" screeched the dame, "what's in the man?"

"Comfort and joy, vrouw, that's what's in him! Ask Gretel, ask my little music box Gretel if your man has lacked comfort and joy this day."

"Not he, Mother," laughed Gretel. "He's been *my* music box, too. We sang together half the time you were gone."

"Aye, so," said the dame, greatly relieved. Now, Hans, you'll never get enough with a piece like that. Here, Gretel, take another slice of the sausage; it'll put blood in your cheeks."

"Oh, Mother!" laughed Gretel, eagerly holding forth her platter, "blood doesn't glow in girls' cheeks. You mean roses — isn't it roses, Hans?"

Before Hans could give a suitable reply, Dame Brinker settled the matter with a quick: "Well, roses or blood, it's all one to me, so the red finds its way on your sunny face."

After dinner, the affair of the watch and its mysterious initials were fully talked over.

Hans had just pushed back his stool, intending to start for Mynheer van Holp's, and his mother had risen to put the watch away, when someone knocked at the door, opening it at the same time.

"Come in," stammered Dame Brinker, hastily trying to hide the watch in her bosom. "Oh, it is you, Doctor Boekman! Good day! The father is nearly well, as you see. It's a poor place to greet you in, mynheer, and the dinner not cleared away."

Dr. Boekman scarcely noticed the Dame's apology. He was evidently in haste.

"Ahem!" he exclaimed, "not needed here, I perceive. The patient is mending fast."

"Well he may, mynheer," cried the dame, "for only

last night we found a thousand guilders that's been
lost to us these ten years."

Dr. Boekman opened his eyes.

"Yes, mynheer," said Raff. "I bid the vrouw tell
you, though it's to be held a secret among us, for I
see you can keep your lips closed as well as any man."

The doctor scowled. He disliked personal remarks.

"Now, mynheer," continued Raff. "you can take
your rightful pay. God knows you have earned it, if
bringing such a poor tool back to the world and his
family can be called a service. Tell the vrouw what's
to pay, mynheer; she will hand out the sum right
willingly."

"Tut-tut!" said the doctor kindly. "Say nothing
about money. I can find plenty of such pay any
time, but gratitude comes seldom. That boy's 'thank
you,' he added, nodding sidewise toward Hans, "was
pay enough for me."

"Like enough ye have a boy of your own," said
Dame Brinker, quite delighted to see the great man
becoming so sociable.

Dr. Boekman's good nature vanished at once. He
gave a growl (at least it seemed so to Gretel), but
made no actual reply.

"Do not think the vrouw meddlesome, mynheer,"
said Raff. "She has been sore touched of late about a
lad whose folks have gone away, none know where;
and I had a message for them from the young gentleman."

"The name was Boomphoffen," said the dame eagerly. "Do you know aught of the family, mynheer?"

The doctor's reply was brief and gruff.

"Yes. A troublesome set. They went long since to America."

"It might be, Raff," persisted Dame Brinker timidly, "that the doctor knows somebody in that country. If he could get the watch to the Boomphoffens with the poor lad's message, it would be a most blessed thing."

"Tut, vrouw, why pester the good doctor, and dying men and women wanting him everywhere? How do ye know ye have the true name?"

"I'm sure of it," she replied. "They had a son Lambert, and there's an L for Lambert and a B for Boomphoffen on the back; though to be sure there's an odd J too, but the doctor can look for himself."

So saying, she drew forth the watch.

"L. J. B.!" cried Dr. Boekman, springing toward her.

Why attempt to describe the scene that followed? I need only say that the lad's message was delivered to his father at last — delivered while the great surgeon sobbed like a child.

"Laurens! My Laurens!" he cried, gazing at the watch as he held it tenderly in his palm. "Ah, if I had but known sooner! Laurens a homeless wanderer — great Heavens! he may be suffering, dying at this moment! Think, man, where is he? Where did my boy say the letter must be sent?"

Raff shook his head sadly.

"Think!" implored the doctor. Surely the memory so lately awakened through his aid could not refuse to serve him in a moment like this.

"It is all gone, mynheer," sighed Raff.

Hans, forgetting distinctions of rank and station, forgetting everything but that his good friend was in trouble, threw his arms round the doctor's neck.

"I can find your son, mynheer. If alive, he is *somewhere*. I will devote every day of my life to the search. Mother can spare me now. You are rich, mynheer; send me where you will."

Gretel began to cry. It was right for Hans to go, but how could they ever live without him?

Dr. Boekman made no reply; neither did he push Hans away. His eyes were fixed anxiously upon Raff Brinker. Suddenly he lifted the watch, and with trembling eagerness attempted to open it. Its stiffened spring yielded at last; the case flew open, disclosing a watch paper in the back bearing a group of blue forget-me-nots. Raff, seeing a shade of intense disappointment pass over the doctor's face, hastened to say:

"There was something else in it, mynheer, but the young gentleman tore it out before he handed it to me. I saw him kiss it as he put it away."

"It was his mother's picture," moaned the doctor. "She died when he was ten years old. Both dead?

It is impossible!" he cried, starting up. "My boy is alive. You shall hear his story:

"Laurens acted as my assistant. By mistake he portioned out the wrong medicine for one of my patients — a deadly poison. It was never administered, for I discovered the error in time. But even so, the man died that same day. I was detained with other bad cases until the next evening. When I reached home my boy was gone.

"Poor Laurens," cried the doctor, "never to hear from me through all these years. His message disregarded. Oh, what he must have suffered!"

Dame Brinker ventured to speak. Anything was better than to see the doctor cry.

"It is a mercy to know the young gentleman was innocent. Ah! how he fretted! Telling you, Raff, that his crime was like unto murder. It was sending the wrong physic he meant. Crime indeed! Why, our own Gretel might have done that! Like enough the poor young gentleman heard that the man was dead— that's why he ran, mynheer. He said, you know, Raff, that he never could come back to Holland again unless" — she hesitated — "ah, your honor, ten years is a dreary time to be waiting to hear from — "

"Hist, vrouw!" said Raff sharply.

"Waiting to hear," groaned the doctor, "and I, like a fool, sitting stubbornly at home, thinking he had abandoned me. I never dreamed, Brinker, that the

boy had discovered the mistake. I believed it was
youthful folly — ingratitude — love of adventure — that
sent him away. My poor, poor Laurens!"

"But you know all now, mynheer," whispered Hans.
"You know he was innocent of wrong, that he loved
you and his dead mother. We will find him. You shall
see him again, dear doctor."

"God bless you!" said Dr. Boekman, seizing the
boy's hand. "It may be as you say. I shall try — I shall
try — and, Brinker, if ever the faintest gleam of recol-
lection concerning him should come to you, you will
send me word at once?"

"Indeed we will!" cried all but Hans, whose silent
promise would have satisfied the doctor even had
the others not spoken.

"Your boy's eyes," he said, turning to Dame
Brinker, "are strangely like my son's. The first time I
met him it seemed that Laurens himself was looking
at me."

"Aye, mynheer," replied the mother proudly. "I
have marked that you were much drawn to the child."

For a few moments the doctor seemed lost in
thought; then, arousing himself, he spoke in a new
voice:

"Forgive me, Raff Brinker, for this tumult. Do not
feel distressed on my account. I leave your house
today a happier man than I have been for many a long
year. Shall I take the watch?"

"Certainly you must, mynheer. It was your son's wish."

"Even so," responded the doctor, regarding his treasure, "even so. And now I must be gone. No medicine is needed by my patient; only peace and cheerfulness, and both are here in plenty. Heaven bless you, my good friends! I shall ever be grateful to you."

"May Heaven bless you, too, mynheer, and may you soon find the dear young gentleman," said Dame Brinker, hurriedly wiping her eyes upon the corner of her apron.

Raff uttered a hearty "Amen!" And Gretel threw such a wistful, eager glance at the doctor that he patted her head as he turned to leave the cottage.

Hans went out also.

"When I can serve you, mynheer, I am ready."

"Very well, boy," replied Dr. Boekman. "Tell them within to say nothing of what has just passed. Meantime, Hans, when you are with your father, watch his mood. You have tact. At any moment he may suddenly be able to tell us more."

"Trust me for that, mynheer."

"Good day, my boy!" cried the doctor, as he sprang into his stately coach.

31. The Great Day Arrives

THE TWENTIETH OF DECEMBER came at last, bringing with it the perfection of winter weather. All over the level landscape lay the warm sunlight, on lake, canal, and river; but the ice showed no sign of melting. The windmills rocked lazily in the clear, still air.

Long before noon the millers near Broek decided to take in their sails and go to the race. Everybody would be there — already the north side of the frozen Y was bordered with eager spectators; the news of the great skating match had traveled far and wide. Men, women, and children in holiday attire were flocking toward the spot. Some wore furs and wintry cloaks or shawls.

The site selected for the race was a faultless plain of ice near Amsterdam, on that great arm of the Zuider Zee called the Eye. Townspeople and strangers alike turned out to see the race.

There were the gentry in their coaches and Amsterdam children in charity uniforms. There were old-fashioned gentlemen in cocked hats and velvet knee breeches, and old-fashioned ladies in stiff, quilted skirts, accompanied by servants bearing foot stoves and cloaks. There were the peasants — shy young rustics, simple village maidens, and women in striped skirts and windmill bonnets. Men wore leather, homespun, velvet, and broadcloth clothes. Burghers appeared in European attire, or in short jackets, wide trousers, and steeple-crowned hats.

There were beautiful Friesland girls in wooden shoes and coarse skirts, their heads encircled with solid gold crescents and hung with lace a century old. Some wore necklaces, pendants, and earrings of the purest gold; many a Friesland woman carried all the family treasure in her headgear.

Scattered throughout the crowd were men from the Island of Marken, wearing sabots, black stockings, and the widest of breeches. The Marken women were dressed in short blue skirts and black jackets, gaily figured in front, with white aprons and caps like a bishop's miter over their golden hair.

The children often were as quaint as their elders, and seemed to have stepped bodily out of old Dutch paintings.

They came from every known town in Holland. There were Utrecht waterbearers, Gouda cheesemakers, Delft pottery-men, Schiedam distillers, Amster-

dam diamond-cutters, Rotterdam merchants, and two
sleepy-eyed shepherds from Texel.

Look at those boys and girls on stilts; they can see
over the heads of the tallest. And listen to the din!
All made up of human voices — well, the horses are
helping somewhat, and the fiddles are squeaking, but
the mass of sound comes from the crowd itself.

High up in the center of one pavilion, erected upon
the border of the ice, is Madame van Gleck. It is her
birthday, and she has the post of honor. There is
Mynheer van Gleck, whose meerschaum pipe appears
to have grown fast to his lips. Grandfather and Grandmother and all the children are there too.

Grandfather, with his pipe and spectacles and fur
cap, makes quite a picture as he holds the baby on his
knee. Perched high on their canopied platforms, the
party can see all that is going on. The ladies look
complacently at the ice; no wonder — with a stove for
a footstool one might sit cozily at the North Pole.

Nearby, in the next pavilion, sit the van Holps with
their son and daughter, the van Gends from the
Hague. Peter's sister has not forgotten her promise,
and she has brought bouquets of exquisite hothouse
flowers for the winners.

These pavilions, and others besides, have all been
erected since dawn. The van Glecks's — the center
one — is striped red and white, and hung with ever-
greens.

The one with the blue flags contains the musicians.

The pagodalike affairs, decked with sea shells and many-colored streamers, are the judges' stands. Two white columns, connected at the top by a strip of drapery, form the starting point. Two flagstaffs, half a mile off, stand at each end of the race course. The boundary line is cut sufficiently deep to be distinct to the skaters, though not enough to trip them as they turn to come back to the starting point.

Now the music has commenced. The racers, assembled near the white columns, are a beautiful sight. Forty boys and girls in picturesque attire dart swiftly in and out, or glide in pairs and triplets, beckoning and chatting. A few careful ones are soberly tightening their straps; others, halting on one leg, suddenly cross a suspected skate over their knee, give it an examining shake, and dart off again. One and all are possessed with the spirit of motion and cannot stand still; their skates seem bewitched.

Holland is the place for skaters. Where else can nearly every boy and girl perform feats on the ice that would attract a crowd if seen in New York City's Central Park? Ben is really astonishing the natives with his skating — no easy thing to do in the Netherlands. Now other boys are trying! Ben is surpassed already. Such jumping, such spinning! That boy with a red cap — he is a bird, a top, a rabbit, a corkscrew, all in an instant. He drops his glove on the ice and turns a somersault as he picks it up. Without stopping, he snatches the cap from Jacob Poot's astonished head and claps it back on again. Yet superb skater that he is, he may lose the race!

There are some familiar faces near the white columns. Lambert, Ludwig, Peter, and Carl are all there, cool and in good skating order. Hans is not far off. Evidently he is going to join in the race, after all, for his skates are on — the very pair that he sold for seven guilders! He had soon suspected that his "fairy godmother" was the mysterious buyer; he had boldly charged Annie with her deed. And she, knowing well that all her little savings had been spent in the purchase, had not had the face to deny it. When Hans found the pot of money with the help of this same "fairy godmother," he was easily able to buy his skates back again. Therefore, he is one of the twenty boys in the race.

Twenty boys and twenty girls. The girls, by this time, are standing in front, braced for the start, for they are to have the first "run." Hilda, Rychie, and Katrinka are among them. Hilda is speaking pleasantly to a graceful little creature in a red jacket and a new skirt. It is Gretel! What a difference those pretty shoes make, and the skirt and the new cap. Annie Bouman is there too.

The race is about to commence.

32. The Race for the Silver Skates

Twenty girls form a line. The rollicking music has ceased.

The crier stands between the columns and the first judges' stand. He reads the rules in a loud voice:

> THE GIRLS AND BOYS ARE TO RACE IN TURN UNTIL ONE GIRL AND ONE BOY HAVE WON TWICE. THEY ARE TO START IN A LINE FROM THE COLUMNS, SKATE TO THE FLAGSTAFF LINE, TURN, AND THEN COME BACK TO THE STARTING POINT — THUS MAKING A MILE AT EACH RUN.

A flag is waved from the judges' stand. Madame van Gleck rises in her pavilion. She leans forward with a white handkerchief in her hand. When she drops it, a bugler will give the signal to start.

Now the handkerchief is fluttering to the ground. Hark! They are off!

No. Back again. Their line was not true in passing the judges' stand.

The signal is repeated.

Off again. No mistake this time. How fast they go!

The multitude is quiet for an instant, absorbed in eager, breathless watching.

Then cheers spring up along the line of spectators. Five girls are ahead. Who comes flying back from the boundary mark? Someone in red. There is a blue spot flitting near it, and a dash of yellow nearer still. Spectators at this end of the line strain their eyes and wish they had taken posts nearer the flagstaff.

The wave of cheering comes again. Now we can see — Katrinka is ahead!

She passes the van Holp pavilion. The next is Madame van Gleck's. Hilda shoots past Katrinka, waving her hand to her mother as she passes. Two others are close now, whizzing on like arrows. What is that flash of red and gray? Hurrah, it is Gretel! She too waves her hand. The crowd is cheering, but she hears only her father's voice, "Well done, little Gretel!" Soon Katrinka, with a quick merry laugh, shoots past Hilda. The girl in yellow is gaining now. She passes them all — all except Gretel. The judges lean forward without seeming to lift their eyes from their watches. Cheer after cheer fills the air; the very columns are rocking. Gretel has passed them. She has won!

"GRETEL BRINKER: ONE MILE!" shouts the crier.

The judges nod. They write something on a tablet that each holds in his hand.

While the girls are resting — some crowding eagerly
around our frightened little Gretel, some standing
aside in high disdain — the boys form in a line.

Mynheer van Gleck drops the handkerchief this
time. The buglers give a vigorous blast.

The boys have started!

Halfway already? Did you ever see the like!

A hundred legs flash by in an instant, or so it seems.
What are the people laughing at? Oh, at that stout
boy in the rear. See him go! Just see him! He'll be
down in an instant — no, he won't. Does he know he
is all alone — that the other boys are nearly at the
boundary line? Yes, he knows it. He stops! He wipes
his hot face. He takes off his cap and looks about him.
Better to give up with good grace. He has made a
hundred friends by that hearty, astonished laugh.
Good Jacob Poot! He is already among the spectators, gazing as eagerly as the rest.

A cloud of feathery ice flies from the heels of the
skaters as they "bring to" and turn at the flagstaffs.

Someone in black is ahead now. The crowd fairly
roars. Now they come nearer — we can see the red
cap. There's Ben — there's Peter — there's Hans!

Hans is ahead! Young Madame van Gend almost
crushes the flowers in her hand; she had been quite
sure that Peter would be first. Carl Schummel is next,
then Ben and the youth with the red cap. The others
are pressing close. A tall figure darts from among
them. He passes the red cap, he passes Ben, then

Carl. Now it is an even race between him and Hans. Madame van Gend catches her breath.

It is Peter! He is ahead! But Hans shoots past him. Hilda's eyes fill with tears; Peter *must* win. Annie's eyes flash proudly. Gretel gazes with clasped hands — four strokes more will take her brother to the columns.

He is there! Yes, but so was young Schummel just a second before. At the last instant, Carl, gathering his powers, whizzes between them and passes the goal.

"CARL SCHUMMEL: ONE MILE!" shouts the crier.

Soon Madame van Gleck rises again. The falling handkerchief starts the bugle, and the sound, like a bowstring, shoots off twenty girls like so many arrows.

It is a beautiful sight, but before one can fairly distinguish them they are far in the distance. This time they are close upon one another; there are new faces among the foremost. Katrinka is there, and Hilda, but Gretel and Rychie are in the rear. Gretel is wavering, but when Rychie passes her, she starts forward afresh. Now they are nearly beside Katrinka. Hilda is still in advance; she is almost "home." She has not faltered since that bugle note sent her flying; like an arrow still, she is speeding toward the goal. Cheer after cheer rises in the air. Peter is silent, but his eyes shine like stars. "Hurrah! Hurrah!"

The crier's voice is heard again:

"HILDA VAN GLECK: ONE MILE!"

A loud murmur of approval runs through the

crowd, catching the music in its course, till all seems
one sound, with a glad rhythmic throbbing in its
depths. When the flag waves, all is still.

Once more the bugle blows a terrific blast. It sends
off the boys like chaff before the wind, driven faster
yet by the cheers and shouts along the line. There
are three boys in advance this time, and all abreast:
Hans, Peter, and Lambert. Carl soon breaks these
ranks, rushing through with a whish! Van Mounen is
flagging, but not Hans or Peter. Peter and Hans:
which one is foremost?

Hilda, Annie, and Gretel, seated upon the long
crimson bench, now spring to their feet, as one in
their eagerness. Hilda instantly reseats herself; none
shall know how anxious, how filled with hope, she is.

"PETER VAN HOLP: ONE MILE!" calls the crier.

The same buzz of excitement as before, while the
judges take notes, the same throbbing of music
through the din — but something is different. A little
crowd presses close about someone lying near the
column. It is Carl, who has fallen. He is not hurt,
though a but stunned. Soon he is on his feet again.

The girls are to skate their third mile.

This third mile may decide the race. Still, if neither
Gretel nor Hilda wins, there is yet a chance among
the rest for the silver skates. Each girl feels sure that
this time she will accomplish the distance in one half
the time, as she stands erect, her eyes on Madame
van Gleck.

The bugle thrills through them again. With quivering eagerness, the girls spring forward, bending but in perfect balance.

Now they are skimming off in the distance. Again the eager straining of eyes, again the shouts and cheering, again the thrill of excitement as four or five, in advance of the rest, come speeding back — nearer, nearer to the white columns.

Who is first? Not Rychie, Katrinka, Annie, Hilda, nor the girl in yellow — but Gretel! Gretel, the fleetest sprite of a girl that ever skated. She was just playing in the earlier race; now she is in earnest. Something within her is determined to win. She cannot stop — not till the goal is passed!

In vain the crier lifts his voice — he cannot be heard. The news he has to tell is already ringing through the crowd. *Gretel has won the silver skates!*

Like a bird she has flown over the ice; like a bird she looks about her in a timid, startled way. She longs to dart to the sheltered nook where her mother and father stand. But Hans is beside her, the girls are crowding round. Hilda's kind, joyous voice breathes in her ear. From that hour, none will despise her. Gretel stands acknowledged Queen of the Skaters!

With natural pride, Hans turned to see if Peter van Holp was witnessing his sister's triumph. Peter was not looking toward them at all. He was kneeling, bending his troubled face low and working hastily

at his skate strap. Hans was beside him at once. "Are
you in trouble, mynheer?"

"Ah, Hans, that you? Yes, my fun is over. I tried
to tighten my strap, to make a new hole, and this
botheration of a knife has cut it nearly in two."

"Mynheer," said Hans, at the same time pulling
off a skate, "you must use my strap!"

"No indeed, Hans Brinker," cried Peter, looking up,
"though I thank you warmly. Go to your post, my
friend; the bugle will sound in a minute."

"Mynheer," pleaded Hans in a husky voice, "if I
am your friend, then take this strap — quick! There
is not an instant to lose. I shall not skate this time;
indeed I am out of practice. Mynheer, you *must* take
it" — and Hans, blind and deaf to any remonstrance,
slipped his strap into Peter's skate.

"Come, Peter!" cried Lambert, from the line. "We
are waiting for you."

"For Madame's sake," pleaded Hans, "be quick.
She is motioning to you to join the racers. There, the
skate is almost on; quick, mynheer, fasten it. I could
not possibly win. The race lies between Schummel
and yourself."

"You are a noble fellow, Hans!" cried Peter, yield-
ing at last. He sprang to his post just as the white
handkerchief fell to the ground.

Now the bugle sends forth its blast again, loud,
clear, and ringing. Off go the boys!

"Good Heavens!" cries a tough old fellow from Delft. "They beat everything, these Amsterdam youngsters. See them go!"

See them, indeed! What mad errand are they on? Are they hunting Peter van Holp? But now Carl is the runaway; the pursuit grows more furious, and Ben is foremost! The chase turns in a cloud of mist. It is coming this way. Who is being hunted now? It is Peter — Peter van Holp. His mother and sister are pale with eagerness. Hilda is trembling and dares not look up. The crowd is cheering madly. The pursurers are close upon him.

"Hurrah! Hurrah! Peter has won the silver skates!"

"PETER VAN HOLP!" shouts the crier.

"Peter van Holp!" shout a hundred voices, for he is the favorite. "Hurrah! Hurrah!"

Now the music strikes up a lively air, then a tremendous march. The spectators, seeing that something new is about to happen, settle down to watch.

The racers form a single file. Peter, being the tallest, stands first. Gretel, the smallest of all, takes her place at the end. Hans, who has borrowed a strap, is near the head. Three gaily twined arches are placed at intervals upon the river facing the van Gleck pavilion. Skating slowly, and in perfect time to the music, the boys and girls move forward, led by Peter.

It is beautiful to see the bright procession glide along like one living creature. It curves and doubles, and draws its graceful length in and out among the arches — whichever way Peter, the head, goes, the body follows. Sometimes it steers direct for the center arch; then it unwinds slowly and, bending low, with quick, snakelike curvings, crosses the river to pass through the farthest arch. Curling, twisting, turning, never losing form until, at the shrill call of the bugle rising above the music, it suddenly resolves itself into boys and girls standing in double semicircle before Madame van Gleck's pavilion.

Peter and Gretel stand in the center, in advance of the others. Madame van Gleck rises majestically. Gretel trembles, but feels that she must look at the beautiful lady. She is thinking that she ought to try and make a curtsy, such as her mother makes to the doctor, when suddenly something so dazzling is placed in her hand that she gives a cry of joy.

Then she ventures to look about her. Peter, too, has something in his hands. "Oh, how splendid!" she cries, and "Oh, how splendid!" is echoed as far as the people can see. Meantime the silver skates flash in the sunshine, throwing dashes of light upon those two happy faces.

Mevrouw van Gend sends a little messenger with her bouquets. One for Hilda and one for Gretel.

At sight of the flowers, the Queen of the Skaters is overwhelmed. With a bright stare of gratitude, she gathers skates and bouquet in her apron, hugs them to her bosom, and darts off to search for her father and mother in the scattering crowd.

33. Joy in the Cottage

HAPPILY, Raff and his vrouw were at the skating race on that merry twentieth of December. That evening the Brinker cottage, standing alone on the frozen marsh, outwardly gave no hint of the lively scene passing within.

Delicious odors filled the air. A huge peat fire on the hearth sent its flickering light over the somber walls. It played in turn on the great leather Bible, the kitchenware, the beautiful silver skates, the flowers on the table, and on Dame Brinker's glowing face. Gretel and Hans were sitting near the fire, laughing merrily, and Raff Brinker was dancing!

At least, while the family were chatting pleasantly together, Raff suddenly sprang from his seat, snapped his fingers, and performed two or three flourishes, much like a Highland fling. Next he caught his vrouw in his arms and fairly lifted her from the ground.

"Hurrah!" he cried, "I have it! I have it! It's Thomas Higgs. That's the name! It came to me like a flash. Write it down, lad, write it down!"

Someone knocked at the door.

"It's the doctor," cried the delighted dame.

"Dear me! How things come to pass!" Mother and children collided merrily as they rushed to open the door.

It was not the doctor, after all, but three boys: Peter von Holp, Lambert, and Ben.

"Good evening, young gentlemen," said Dame Brinker, so happy and proud that she would scarcely have been surprised at a visit from the king himself.

"Good evening, juffrouw," said the trio, making magnificent bows.

"Pray be seated, young masters" said the dame, as Gretel bashfully thrust a stool toward them. "There's a lack of chairs as you see, but this one by the fire is at your service, and if you don't mind the hardness, the oak chest is as good a seat as the best. That's right, Hans, pull it out."

By the time the boys were seated to the dame's satisfaction, Peter, acting as spokesman, had explained that they were going to attend a lecture at Amsterdam and had stopped on the way to return Hans's strap.

"Oh, mynheer," cried Hans, "it was most kind of you to trouble."

"No trouble at all, Hans. I could have waited for you to come to your work tomorrow, had I not wished to call. And, Hans, talking of your work, my father is much pleased with it; a carver by trade could not have done better. He would like to have the south arbor ornamented also, but I told him you were going to school again."

"Aye!" put in Raff Brinker emphatically. "Hans must go to school at once, and Gretel as well — that is true."

"I am glad to hear you say so," responded Peter, turning toward the father, "and very glad to know that you are again a well man."

"Yes, young master, a well man, and able to work as steady as ever — thank God!"

Meanwhile, Hans was hastily writing something on the edge of a time-worn almanac that hung by the chimney place.

"Aye, that's right, lad, set it down. Figgs? Wiggs? Alack, alack!" added Raff in great dismay, "it's gone again!"

"All right, Father," said Hans, "the name's down now in black and white. Here, look at it, Father; mayhap the rest will come to you. If we had the place as well, the address would be complete." Then, turning to Peter, he said in a low tone, "I have an important errand in town, mynheer, and if —"

"Whist!" exclaimed the dame, lifting her hands, "not to Amsterdam tonight! It'll be soon enough to go at early daylight."

"Daylight indeed!" echoed Raff. "That would never do. Nay, Meitje, he must go this hour."

"Very well, Raff," she said smilingly.

Peter drew a long strap from his pocket. Handing
it to Hans, he said in an undertone, "I must say you
did me a great kindness, Hans Brinker. I did not
know," he added laughingly, "until I was in the race,
how anxious I was to win."

Hans was glad to join in Peter's laugh; it covered
his embarrassment.

"It was nothing, mynheer," said the dame, hastening to her son's relief. "The lad was all for having
you win the race — I know he was."

"Ah, mynheer," Hans hurried to say, "from the
first start I felt stiff and strange on my feet; I was well
out of it, as long as I had no chance of winning."

Peter looked distressed. "We may hold different
opinions there. That part of the business troubles
me. It is too late to mend it now, but it would be
a real kindness to me if —"

The rest of Peter's speech could not be heard.
Enough to say, Hans started back in dismay, and
Peter, looking rather embarrassed, stammered out
that he would keep them, since he had won the race,
but that it was "all wrong."

Here van Mounen coughed, to remind Peter that
the lecture hour was fast approaching. At the same
time Ben laid a red leather box on the table.

"Ah," exclaimed Peter, "I forgot my other errand.
Your sister ran off so quickly today that Madame
van Gleck had no opportunity to give her the case
for her skates."

"S-s-t!" said Dame Brinker, shaking her head reproachfully at Gretel. "She was a very rude girl, I'm sure."

"No, indeed," laughed Peter, "she did exactly the right thing: ran home with her richly won treasure. Who would not? Don't let us detain you, Hans," he continued, turning around as he spoke; but Hans, who was watching the father, seemed to have forgotten their presence.

Raff was repeating under his breath, "Thomas Higgs, Thomas Higgs — aye, that's the name. Alack! If I could but tell the place as well."

Gretel was clutching the skate case tightly. It was elegantly made of crimson morocco, ornamented in silver, with *"For the Fleetest"* written on the cover in sparkling letters, and lined with velvet. In one corner was stamped the name and address of the maker.

Gretel had thanked Peter in her own simple way; then, being quite delighted and confused, and not knowing what else to do, lifted the case, carefully examining it in every part. "It's made by Mynheer Birmingham," she said after a while, still blushing and holding it close.

"Birmingham!" replied Lambert van Mounen, "that's the name of a place in England. Let me see it."

"Ha, ha!" he laughed, holding the open case toward the firelight, "no wonder you thought so; but it's a slight mistake. The case was made at Birmingham, but the maker's name is in smaller letters. Humph! They're so small, I can't read them."

"Let me try," said Peter, leaning over his shoulder. "Why, man, it's perfectly distinct. It's T-H-"

"Well," exclaimed Lambert triumphantly, "if you can read it so easily, let's hear it — T-H what?"

"TH— Oh! Why, THOMAS HIGGS, to be sure," replied Peter, pleased to be able to decipher it at last. Then he turned toward Hans.

But what was the matter with these people? Raff and Hans had started up and were staring at Peter in glad amazement. Gretel looked wild. Dame Brinker, with an unlighted candle in her hand, was rushing about the room crying, "Hans! Hans! Where's your hat? Oh, the doctor! The doctor!"

"Birmingham! Higgs!" exclaimed Hans. "Did you say Higgs? We've found him! I must be off."

"You see, young masters," panted the dame, at the same time snatching Hans's hat from the bed. "you see — we know him — he's — I mean — oh, Hans, you must go to Amsterdam this minute!"

"Good night, mynheers," panted Hans, radiant with sudden joy, "good night. You will excuse me, I must go. Birmingham — Higgs, Higgs — Birmingham," and seizing his hat from his mother and his skates from Gretel, he rushed from the cottage.

What could the boys think, but that the entire Brinker family had suddenly gone crazy!

They bade an embarrassed "good evening" and turned to go. But Raff stopped them.

"This Thomas Higgs, young masters, is a — a person."

"Ah!" said Peter.

"Yes — a person — a — ahem! — a friend. We thought him dead. I hope it is the same man. In England, did you say?"

"Yes, Birmingham," answered Peter. "It must be Birmingham in England."

"I know the man," said Ben, addressing Lambert. "His factory is not four miles from our place. A queer fellow, still as an oyster — he doesn't seem at all like an Englishman. I've often seen him: a solemn-looking chap with magnificent eyes. He made a beautiful writing case once for me to give Jenny on her birthday. Makes pocketbooks, telescope cases, and all kinds of leatherwork."

As this was said in English, van Mounen of course translated it for the benefit of all concerned, noticing meanwhile that although neither Raff nor his vrouw looked unhappy, Raff was trembling, and the dame's eyes were swimming with tears.

You may believe the doctor heard every word of the story, when later in the evening he came driving back with Hans.

"The three young gentlemen have been gone some

time," Dame Brinker said, "but like enough, by hurrying, it would be easy to find them coming out from the lecture, wherever that was."

"True," said Raff, nodding his head, "the vrouw always hits upon the right thing. It would be well to see the young English gentleman, mynheer, before he forgets all about Thomas Higgs. It came upon me sudden and strong as a pile driver, and my boy writ it down. Aye, mynheer, I'd haste to talk with the English lad; he's seen your son many a time — only to think on't!"

Dame Brinker took up the thread of the discourse: "You'll pick out the lad quick enough, mynheer, because he's in company with Master Peter van Holp; and his hair curls all up over his forehead like foreign folks's; and if you hear him speak, he talks kind of big and fast, only it's English — but that wouldn't be any hindrance to your honor."

The doctor had already lifted his hat to go. With a beaming face, he muttered something about its being just like the young scamp to give himself a rascally English name; called Hans "my son," thereby making that young gentleman happy as a lord; and left the cottage with very little ceremony, considering what a great doctor he was.

34. The Mysterious Disappearance of Thomas Higgs

Hıggs's FACTORY was a mine of delight for the gossips of Birmingham. It was a small building, but quite large enough to hold a mystery. Who the proprietor was, or where he came from, none could tell. He looked like a gentleman, that was certain, though everybody knew he had risen from an apprenticeship, and he could handle his pen like a writing master.

Years ago he had suddenly appeared in the place — a lad of eighteen, who learned his trade faithfully and had risen in the confidence of his employer. He had been taken in as a partner soon after his time was up, and finally, when old Willett died, had assumed the business himself. But this was all anyone knew of his affairs.

Some people claimed that he never had a word to say; others declared that he spoke beautifully, when he chose to, but that he had a strange accent.

His nationality was a great puzzle. The English

name spoke plain enough for one side of his house, but what of his mother? Was that side American? German? French? No — there was nothing it could be but Dutch. But though the man always pricked up his ears when you talked of Holland, he didn't seem to know the first thing about the country. No letters ever came to him from Holland, and nobody living had ever seen old Higgs. Thus Thomas Higgs and his affairs were never-failing subjects of discussion.

Picture, then, the consternation among all the good people when it was announced by "somebody who was there and ought to know" that the postboy had that very morning· handed Higgs a foreign-looking letter, and the man had "turned as white as the wall, rushed to his factory, talked a bit with one of the head workmen, and, without bidding a creature good-bye, was off bag and baggage before you could wink."

An investigating committee met that evening in Mrs. Snigham's parlor — sitting in a secret session over her best china. Though invited only to a quiet tea, the amount of business they transacted on the occasion was enormous. The biscuits were actually cold before the committee had a chance to eat anything. There was so much to talk over, and it was so important to establish firmly that each member had always been "certain sure something extraordinary would be happening to the man yet," that it was nearly eight o'clock before Mrs. Snigham gave anybody a second cup of tea.

35. Broad Sunshine

ONE SNOWY DAY IN JANUARY, Laurens Boekman went with his father to pay his respects to the Brinker family.

Raff was resting after the labors of the day; Gretel, having filled and lighted his pipe, was brushing every speck of ash from the hearth. The dame was spinning; and Hans, perched upon a stool by the window, was diligently studying his lessons. It was a peaceful, happy household, whose main excitement during the past week had been looking forward to this visit from Thomas Higgs.

As soon as the introductions were over, Dame Brinker insisted upon giving her guests some hot tea; it was enough to freeze anyone, she said, to be out in such blustering weather. While they were talking with her husband, she whispered to Gretel that the young gentleman's eyes and her boy's were certainly alike, to say nothing of a way they both had of looking as if they were stupid and yet knowing as much as a body's grandfather.

Gretel was disappointed. She had looked forward to a tragic scene such as Annie Bouman had often described to her from storybooks; yet here he was — the gentleman who had come so near being a murderer, who for ten years had been wandering over the face of the earth, and who had believed himself deserted and scorned by his father. This very same young gentleman, who had fled from his country in such magnificent trouble, was now sitting by their fire, looking as pleasant and natural as any ordinary person.

Yes, Gretel was disappointed. But not Raff. He was quite satisfied. His message had been delivered; Dr. Boekman had his son back safe and sound; and the poor lad had done nothing sinful after all, except in thinking his father would ever have abandoned him because of an accident. To be sure, the youth had become rather a heavy man. Raff had hoped to clasp that same boyish hand again; but then, all things were changed.

Hans, meantime, was thinking of Thomas Higgs's probable happiness in being the doctor's assistant again; and Dame Brinker was sighing softly to herself, wishing that the lad's mother were alive to see him today.

The light shone full on Dr. Boekman's face. How contented he looked, how much younger and brighter. The hard lines were quite melting away. He was laughing as he said, "Am I not a happy man,

Raff Brinker? My son will sell out his factory in England this month and open a warehouse in Amsterdam. I shall get all my spectacle cases for nothing."

Hans started from his reverie. "A warehouse, mynheer! And will Thomas Higgs — I mean, is your son not to be your assistant again?"

A shade passed over the doctor's face, but he brightened with an effort, as he replied, "Oh no, Laurens has had quite enough of that. He wishes to be a merchant."

Hans appeared so surprised and disappointed that the doctor asked good-naturedly, "Why so silent, boy? Is it any disgrace to be a merchant?"

"N— not a disgrace, mynheer," stammered Hans, "but — "

"But what?"

"Why, the other calling is so much better," answered Hans, "so much nobler. I think, mynheer," he added, kindling with enthusiasm, "that to be a surgeon, to cure the sick and crippled, to save human life, to be able to do what you have done for my father, is the grandest thing on earth."

The doctor was regarding him sternly. Hans's cheeks flushed. He felt rebuked.

"It is an ugly business, boy, this surgery," said the doctor, still frowning at Hans. "It requires great patience, self-denial, and perseverance."

"I am sure it does," cried Hans, kindling again. "It calls for wisdom, too, and a reverence for God's

work. Ah, mynheer, it may have its trials and draw-
backs, but you do not mean what you say — it is great
and noble, not ugly! Pardon me, mynheer. It is not
for me to speak so boldy."

Dr. Boekman was evidently displeased. He turned
his back on the boy and conferred aside with Laurens.
Meanwhile the dame scowled a terrible warning at
Hans. These great people, she knew well enough,
never liked to hear poor folk speak up so pertly.

The doctor turned around.

"How old are you, Hans Brinker?"

"Fifteen, mynheer," was the startled reply.

"Would you like to become a physician?"

"Yes, mynheer," answered Hans, quivering with
excitement.

"Would you be willing, with your parents' consent,
to devote yourself to study, to go to the university,
and in time be a student in my office?"

"*Yes*, mynheer."

"You would not grow restless, think you, and
change your mind just as I had set my heart upon
preparing you to be my successor?"

Hans' eyes flashed. "No, mynheer, I would not
change."

"You may believe him there," cried the dame, who
could remain quiet no longer. "Hans is like a rock
when once he makes up his mind; and as for study,
mynheer, the child has almost grown fast to his books

of late. He can rattle off Latin already like any priest!"

The doctor smiled. "Well, Hans, I see nothing to prevent us from carrying out this plan, if your father agrees."

"Ahem," said Raff, too proud of his boy to be very meek. "The fact is, mynheer, I prefer an active, out-door life, myself. But if the lad's inclined to study for a doctor, and he'd have the benefit of your good word to push him on in the world, it's all one to me. The money's all that's wanting, but it mightn't be long, with two strong pairs of arms to earn it, before we —"

"Tut-tut!" interrupted the doctor, "if I take your right-hand man away, I must pay the cost, and glad enough will I be to do it. It will be like having *two* sons, eh, Laurens? One a merchant and the other a surgeon. I shall be the happiest man in Holland! Come to me in the morning, Hans, and we will arrange matters at once."

Hans bowed assent. He dared not trust himself to speak.

"And, Brinker," continued the doctor, "my son Laurens will need a trusty, ready man like you when he opens his warehouse in Amsterdam; someone to oversee matters, and see that the lazy clowns round the place do their duty. Someone to — why don't you tell him yourself, you rascal!"

This last was addressed to the son, and did not sound half as fierce as it looks in print. The rascal and Raff soon understood each other perfectly.

"I'm loath to leave the dykes," said the latter, after they had talked together a while, "but you have made me such a good offer, mynheer, I'd be robbing my family if I let it go."

Take a long look at Hans as he sits there staring gratefully at the doctor; you shall not see him again for many years.

And Gretel — ah, what a vista of puzzling work suddenly opens before her! Yes, for dear Hans's sake she will study now. If he really is to be a doctor, his sister must not shame his greatness.

Conclusion

Our story is nearly told. Time passes in Holland just as surely and steadily as it does here.

To the Brinker family, it has brought great changes. Hans has spent the years faithfully, pursuing one object with all the energy of his nature. Sometimes he echoes, with his good old friend, the words said long ago in that little cottage near Broek: "Surgery is an ugly business"; but always in his heart lingers the echo of those truer words: "It is great and noble! It awakes a reverence for God's work!"

Were you in Amsterdam today, you might see the famous Dr. Brinker driving through the streets to visit his patients; or, it might be, you would see him skating with his own boys and girls upon the frozen canal.

For Annie Bouman, you would inquire in vain: but Annie Brinker, the vrouw of the great physician, is very like her — only, as Hans says, she is even lovelier, wiser, more like a fairy godmother than ever.

Peter van Holp, also, is a married man. He and Hilda joined hands and glide through life together, just as years ago they skimmed side by side over the frozen canal.

Katrinka is single to this day. The lady is not quite so merry as formerly, but she is the life of her social circle still.

Rychie's soul has been stirred to its depths during these long years. In the witty but earnest author whose words and books are welcomed in thousands of Dutch homes, few could recognize the haughty, flippant Rychie who scoffed at little Gretel.

Ludwig van Holp and Lambert van Mounen are good men and thriving citizens. Both live in Amsterdam, one in the old city in Holland, and the other across the ocean in "New Amsterdam," as New York City was once called. Van Mounen's present home is not far from Central Park. When he thinks of the

Katrinka of his boyhood, he is glad that Katrinka
the woman sent him away. Ben's sister Jenny has
made him very happy — happier than he could have
been with anyone else.

Carl Schummel has had a hard life. His father met
with reverses in business; and as Carl had not made
many warm friends, and above all was not sustained
by noble principles, he has been tossed about by
fortune. He is finally settled as a bookkeeper in the
thriving Amsterdam house of Boekman and Schimmelpenninck.

Of all our group of Holland friends, Jacob Poot is
the only one who is not living. Truehearted and un-
selfish to the last, he is mourned now as heartily as
he was loved and laughed at while on earth. He grew
to be very thin before he died — thinner than Benjamin Dobbs, who is now portliest among the portly.

Raff Brinker and his vrouw have been living comfortably in Amsterdam for many years — a faithful,
happy pair, as simple and straightforward in their
good fortune as they were patient and trustful in
darker days. They have a zommerhuis near the old
cottage, and there they spend the pleasant summer
afternoons with their children and grandchildren.

The story of Hans Brinker would be only half told
if we did not leave him with Gretel standing near.
Dear, quick, patient little Gretel! What is she now?
Ask old Dr. Boekman: he will declare she is the finest

singer, the loveliest woman in Amsterdam. Ask Hans
and Annie: they will assure you she is the dearest
sister who ever lived. Ask her husband: he will tell
you she is the brightest, sweetest wife in Holland.
Ask Dame Brinker and Raff: their eyes will glisten
with joyous tears. Ask the poor: the air will be filled
with their blessings.

But Hilda van Holp has never forgotten a tiny
form trembling and sobbing on the mound before the
Brinker cottage. And the van Glecks never weary of
telling about the little girl who won the silver skates.